Some jobs are just too good to be true.

Captain Matt Spears learns this the ... employer hires his ship to hunt down an ... on providing his own pilot. Ryce Faine is ... has rarely met anyone more obnoxious. With tensions running high, it isn't until they are attacked by the hostile Alraki that Matt grudgingly begins to respect Ryce's superior skills, respect that transforms into a tentative attraction.

Little did he know that their biggest challenge would be reaching their destination, an abandoned alien base located on a distant moon amid a dense asteroid field. But when Matt learns that Ryce isn't completely who he says he is and the artifact is more than he bargained for, he is faced with a difficult choice. One that might change the balance of forces in the known galaxy.

Matt doesn't take well to moral dilemmas; he prefers the easy way out. But that might not be possible anymore, when his past comes back to haunt him at the worst possible moment. When faced with a notorious pirate carrying a personal grudge, the fragile connection Matt has formed with Ryce might be the only thing that he can count on to save them both.

This is a work of fiction. All characters, places and events are from the author's imagination and should not be confused with fact. Any resemblance to persons, living or dead, events or places is purely coincidental.

Copyright 2017 by Isabelle Adler

All rights reserved, including the right of reproduction in whole or in part in any form.

Published by
NineStar Press
PO Box 91792
Albuquerque, New Mexico, 87199
www.ninestarpress.com

Print ISBN #978-1-945952-55-5
Cover by Natasha Snow
Edited by Elizabetta

No part of this publication may be reproduced in any material form, whether by printing, photocopying, scanning or otherwise without the written permission of the publisher, NineStar Press, LLC

Adrift

Staying Afloat, Book 1

Isabelle Adler

DEDICATION

To my friends Jack and Maria, without whom there would be no story.

Chapter One

"No way," Matt said. "No way in hell."

The low hum of music and the loud voices threatened to swallow his response. The Blue Giant was like any other canteen on any other small-time maintenance space station, offering cheap drinks and free talk, catering to drifters, smugglers, freelance pilots, and the dregs of every known society. The strong smell of synthetic spirits enveloped the crowded room in an almost tangible cloud. It really wasn't the best location for conducting business, even over interstellar communications channels, but one could stand being cooped up in a spaceship for only so long.

Matt ignored the noise best he could as he squinted at the commlink screen. This wasn't a regular type of job, but then again, freelancers didn't exactly have regular jobs. As it was, this one promised to be very well paying. His potential client had introduced himself as Mr. Ari, though Matt suspected it wasn't his real name. They usually weren't. At the moment, he was more concerned with Mr. Ari's terms and conditions than with his identity, fake or otherwise.

"This is nonnegotiable," Ari said firmly. There was no image on-screen, just his computer-altered voice in the earpiece. "I require that my own pilot navigate your ship to destination. He's the only one who will know the exact route and the details of the mission. I'm merely hiring your ship to transport my man and provide him with assistance."

"It's my ship and I'm the only one flying her," Matt said indignantly. "No way I'll just let some stranger take over. Now, a passenger, that's another matter. I've nothing against passengers, so long as they're nice and quiet." And good-looking, but he wasn't about to say that to the client's face, or to the lack thereof, as the case was. But another pilot? This was ridiculous. If the only thing this guy needed was a ship, there were much simpler alternatives than hiring Matt's services.

"As I've said before, Captain, this job requires subtlety and a very specific set of skills," Ari said. Even with the distortion, he somehow managed to make "Captain" sound like an insult. "Which, with all due respect, I doubt you possess. This is a salvage mission, and the location must remain a secret until you get there. To put it simply, you sit back, let my man do the job, get back safely, and collect the cash—as long as you keep your mouth firmly shut about any of this. I've been told that your ship is fast and well equipped, and that you are discreet. I'd hate to think that I've been misinformed."

Matt took a long sip of his beer to stall for time. The beer had a distinct sour artificial aftertaste, but at least it was cold. "What kind of salvage?"

"An abandoned alien site. I'm afraid I can't divulge further information at this point, other than it would require a jump to another sector."

"Huh," Matt grunted. The guy was definitely too well-spoken to be a scavenger; on the other hand, off-world archaeological salvage (if that was indeed Ari's intent) was usually done for strictly academic purposes and required government permits. Any other form of salvage, whether human or alien, was considered theft and was absolutely illegal. That *and* some other guy had to fly his ship? There was no way in hell he'd agree to that. This Mr. Ari could either fuck off or pay him way more than he was offering. "Well, you make it sound very tempting and all, but still. A pilot has his pride, you know. No one takes my seat, twenty thousand Fed-creds or no."

"Name your price," Ari said tersely.

"One hundred thousand," Matt said, testing the waters.

"Done," Ari said with a finality that left Matt a little dizzy. He was sure Ari would balk at the asking price. He wondered belatedly whether he could have gotten away with being even bolder. "My pilot will meet you at Dock G5 in two hours. You'll get twenty percent of your fee now, and the rest when the job is done."

"Agreed," Matt said. How did this guy know exactly where his ship was? Shit, he could hardly back down on the offer now. "I'll send you the account number."

"Now, Mr. Spears, I must stress again how delicate this assignment is."

"Of course," Matt said. Really, this was tedious. Every client thought they were the only one in the galaxy who had dirty secrets. He wouldn't have been in this line of work for as long as he had if he couldn't keep his mouth shut and his eyes averted.

"You might encounter...competition," Ari said. "While this is unlikely to happen, there is a chance that other parties might try to intercept you."

"What do you mean, 'intercept'?" Matt asked suspiciously. "Just to make it clear—I'm a runner, not a mercenary. If it's something dangerous—"

"The reason I'm not willing to be more specific is precisely because I don't want any information to leak out and pose a threat to your mission," Ari said, sounding a bit too vague for Matt's comfort. "However, you should be on alert, and report any incidents to my agent."

Now he wanted him to report to the guy? Matt was utterly and completely done with reporting to anybody for the rest of his life. He was more than capable of handling any situation, and he wasn't about to play the chain-of-command game with his client's representative. However, he kept it prudently to himself. You didn't sass somebody who was willing to shell out all those credits.

"Got it," he said dryly. "I'll be on alert. Anything else?"

"You may discuss further details with my man, and he'll be handling all future communications. Good luck, Captain."

"My pleasure," Matt said. He disconnected the call and sagged back into his chair, pushing away the beer. He had a very, very bad feeling. Nobody paid this much cash, without haggling, for what looked to be a fairly easy task. Working as a freelance runner—which, to be honest, was just a euphemism for smuggler—meant most of his jobs tended to skirt the law. Over the years, he had developed a keen sense of self-preservation. And right now, it was screaming at him to call Ari back and tell him to go and find himself another ship. But his imagination was no less keen, and it presented him with tempting images of all those big numbers in his account and all those expensive modifications he could now afford to make on his *Lisa*.

He tapped on the screen again, bringing up the video feed.

"Hey Tony," he said as his first mate answered the call. "I think I just landed a new job for us."

"You think?" Tony raised her eyebrows. "You're not sure?"

"I'm still not convinced it's worth taking," Matt answered. "The client promised a shitload of money, but there's something fishy about it. And he wants his guy to run the show. As in going with us and actually flying the ship. You know I hate people telling me what to do."

"Except me," Tony pointed out.

"Except you, hot stuff. But you're the only one who gets away with it."

Tony seemed to consider his misgivings. He usually trusted her judgment, but they both knew perfectly well they couldn't afford to be too picky at the moment. With the increasing Federal presence in the Sonora system, business had been slow lately, and they were running dangerously low on cash.

As a runner, Matt didn't keep a large crew. For the last two years it'd been only him, Tony, and Val manning his little Phaeton cargo vessel, the *Lady Lisa*. Most of the profits went toward keeping the ship operational. Sonora was a busy sector, with lots of competition, so every job was important. It would be foolish to pass on such a lucrative opportunity simply because of Matt's gut feeling. But he knew that if he told Tony he wanted to turn the client down, she'd back him up.

"Are you sure you want to pick up another job right now?" she asked. "We're still not done with our current one, and it's kinda...sensitive."

"Yeah, I remember. But the client doesn't have to know that; and besides, it should work out okay. He wants us to make a long-distance jump, so we'll have to be at Freeport 16 anyway. We drop the cargo like we promised, collect our pay, and make the jump to wherever it is he wants us to go." He paused for a moment. "The thing is, I'm really not sure this job is legit."

"Can't be less legit than what we're doing right now," she pointed out.

"True. But it's not a simple cargo run; it's more like...a scavenger hunt, I think. And he wants to get to the prize first. I don't know; this feels shady. And I'm not keen on letting some nobody on my bridge," he added, just to make this point as clear as possible, in case there was some ambiguity regarding this issue.

Tony thought about it. Between the two of them, she was the rational one, and while he wasn't always prudent enough to heed her advice, this time he was ready to take it to heart.

"At least meet the guy," she said finally. "You can always tell the client you've changed your mind if he rubs you the wrong way."

"I guess it wouldn't hurt," Matt conceded grudgingly. God, he really hated being bossed around. He liked it even less on his own ship. What kind of "specific set of skills" would a pilot need, anyway? This wasn't a Falcon fighter. Hell, most of the time they cruised on autopilot. But a hundred-grand fee was too tempting to turn down because of his ego, even if he was secretly hoping Tony would be against him accepting the offer. "If it's some stupid thug, I say screw it."

Mr. Ari's pilot wasn't a thug.

Matt could see it even on the tiny intercom monitor as the man requested permission to come aboard. He was tall and lean, dressed in nondescript gray fatigues, and carried a duffel bag. Matt sighed as he activated the main hatch switch, and then headed out to meet him.

The man waited patiently for Matt to greet him, looking more like a model in a Blue Dawn Beverage ad than a pilot, with his chiseled cheekbones and eyes the color of storm clouds. Really, this was Ari's point man? This pretty boy was supposed to be a better pilot than him? He didn't look old enough to fly without getting motion sickness. Still, the tiny implants on his temples that enabled connection with a ship's computer looked state of the art. Matt resisted the urge to touch his own, which really needed an upgrade. Maybe now, with Mr. Ari's money, he could finally do it.

"Captain Spears?" the guy asked. There was no trace of youthful eagerness in his voice. If anything, he sounded mildly displeased. Matt wondered if it was with himself, his ship, or the entire situation.

"That's right," Matt said brightly, trying not to let his irritation show and offering his hand. "Welcome aboard *Lady Lisa*, fastest vessel in the Sonora sector. And you are?"

"Ryce Faine," the guy said, making no motion to shake his hand.

"Right," Matt said. "So, you're Mr. Ari's pilot. Have you ever been on a Phaeton spacecraft before?"

"Can't say that I have," Faine muttered, glancing around. Matt carried on, despite Faine's reticence.

"I'll show you around, then. It's pretty simple—just one main deck and a cargo hold below. The engine room is down there too," he said as they walked along the corridor that ran the length of the ship. "We have to deliver our current load at Freeport 16, so after that, we'll use their jumpgate to get to wherever it is we're going. I understand it's supposed to be an interstellar run, right? Here's the galley, and that's Tony— Hey, Tony! Meet Ryce Faine."

Tony was busy brewing something that looked suspiciously like some kind of herbal tea but smelled like old socks. (Really, why anyone would drink it when they had a stock of perfectly fine contraband coffee was beyond him.) She looked up, fixing her sharp dark eyes on Faine inquisitively, and nodded. He nodded politely back.

"Tony is our resident medic, among other things," Matt explained by way of introduction. Truthfully, though, her medical training was incidental at best and so far had been limited to providing first aid when Val burned his fingers on wiring. When Faine didn't respond, Matt added: "She's also the only one of us who can cook, so it pays to be nice to her." He winked at Tony before she could find offense in his statement, and continued down the corridor toward the personal cabins located on the starboard quarter. This area also included a recreation room and a gym. One of the cabins had been converted into an infirmary.

Lady Lisa was originally built for a larger crew, so there were several empty cabins. A ship of this class usually required about six people, but Matt had neither the money nor the inclination to hire more. Three was a nice number. Sometimes it made the operation challenging, especially when they had to carry sensitive cargo, like now, but they always managed to get by somehow. And in their line of work, more people would only mean more unnecessary complications. At least that's what he told himself.

They paused at the entrance to the rec room.

"Do you have any experience with haulers?" Matt asked. But really, what kind of experience could this guy possibly have had? How old was he even? Twenty-two? Twenty-three?

"A bit," Faine said. "I worked on Balius freight vessels for a couple of years, before going into the private transport sector."

"Huh," Matt said. A Balius was a heavy-duty barge, used mainly by mining companies operating in deep space. Flying something like that wouldn't be the most exciting job, but it definitely required some skill.

Granted, Matt wasn't the shrewdest judge of character, but he didn't get the sense that Faine was lying. The guy wasn't friendly, but he wasn't overbearing either; he appeared intelligent, and he was definitely easy on the eyes. There really was no objective reason to send him packing and lose the huge paycheck. Given their present state of affairs, being choosy was not an option. And with their current cargo, they couldn't waste any time on trial runs, testing the new pilot in action.

"I'll show you to your cabin," Matt said, somewhat reluctantly.

The cabins were small, accommodating little more than a bunk bed, a cupboard, and a bathroom, but they allowed for some privacy and came in handy for those passengers who wished to escape unwanted attention.

"There you go," Matt said as the cabin door slid open.

"Thanks," Faine said, passing Matt to enter the room. He dropped his bag on the bunk and looked around the tiny space without comment.

"The bridge is that way," Matt said, pointing down the corridor when the silence stretched into awkwardness. "You can take your time getting further acquainted with the ship. We won't be leaving for a few more hours."

Faine frowned.

"My employer stressed that this is a matter of some urgency," he said.

Matt refrained from rolling his eyes. Who even talked like that?

"This station isn't exactly my favorite hangout in the galaxy. We're here for technical maintenance, and, unfortunately, we're not done with it yet. Once Val, our engineer, gives the all clear, we can go. Besides, we have to stock up on supplies, unless you're cool with eating nothing but protein bars for the rest of the trip."

Faine seemed to accept that, though he still looked dissatisfied. Matt almost told him not to pout.

"Still, I'd like to go over the ship's specs and fill you in on the mission as soon as possible," Faine said. "I'll meet you on the bridge in half an hour, Captain." He nodded and shut the cabin door firmly in Matt's face.

☆☆☆

Tony had almost finished her tea when Matt came into the galley and dropped onto a chair at the round plastic table.

"God, what an uptight asshole," he said with feeling. "This is going to be the longest run in my life."

"Well, you seem to have made up your mind rather quickly. What happened to vetting him?" asked Tony.

"Do we have any choice?" Matt rubbed his face briskly. "We're out of cash; we need the job. I'll have to overlook what a snobbish prick he is."

"He's pretty, though," said Tony, who knew his tastes rather well by now. "I think you decided when you took one look at that fresh face." She grinned at him cheekily. "Who said you can't have some fun while he's here?"

"Does this fun involve strangling him with my bare hands? Because I might be up for that," Matt said. But the prospect of scoring with Mr. Cheekbones did hold an appeal and made him perk up a bit. He didn't consider himself by any means irresistible, but he was reasonably young and attractive. Okay, at thirty-one he wasn't exactly youthful, but his fetchingly green eyes, perpetually tousled auburn hair, and charming personality were enough to enjoy the attention of both sexes. And if Faine wasn't game, well, getting a rise out of him would be entertaining all by itself. It wasn't a very professional thing to do, but Faine wasn't the end client, and they weren't in a formal line of business anyway. "Where's Val?"

Tony shrugged and pulled at her braid. It was long and looked too heavy for her petite figure, but Matt had never seen her sporting any other hairdo.

"He went down to the station. Said something about scoping for a new air compressor. I also told him to pick up some produce at the station mart, if they have it."

"Produce? In this hellhole? The only thing that comes close is the fungus growing in the men's rooms at the canteen."

Tony made a sound of disgust.

"I'm sick of this canned stuff," she complained. "I've been eating nothing but beans and tomato soup for two weeks. A girl needs her vitamins."

"Those are chock-full of vitamins. It says so right on the tin. And you'll have to suffer for only a few more weeks. After we're done with this job, it's vacation time, I promise. You wanted to take that cruise on Nova, didn't you? All the vitamins and sunshine you want."

"Yeah, I've been hearing that a lot."

"But this time it's true," Matt protested. "I told you, if we get this done, there's a big pile of cash waiting for us. Enough to buy us some time off, anyway."

He pulled out his commlink and dialed Val, who answered right away. There were clunking noises in the background, but it was metal against metal, not glass, so he probably wasn't at the canteen. Not that he was the canteen-frequenting type.

"Hey, big guy," Matt said. "Are you done there? I got us a job, and the client is really bent on leaving as soon as possible."

"Yeah, I'm done." Val's voice was booming, even over the commlink. "The tank should be full already. I'll just pick some stuff up and be there in a few."

"Sure thing," said Matt. He disconnected and shoved the comm back in his pocket.

Tony was still watching him.

"What are you gonna do with your time off?" she asked.

"Oh, I don't know. You know me, I'm not a beach party kind of guy."

She huffed, looking at him with some amusement mixed with concern. He didn't really like that look; it usually meant she was going to have a "serious talk," and he hated those.

"Why don't you try calling Nora when it's all over? Her birthday is in three weeks, isn't it?"

Oh God, he was right. "The talk." He leaned back in his chair, folding his arms over his chest.

"Should I ask how you even know when my sister's birthday is?"

"No," Tony said, unfazed. "What you should ask yourself is, 'how long has it been since I've talked with my only sibling?'"

"I know exactly how long it's been, and why." There was no point in getting angry with Tony. After the dream of having her own family fell apart, she was determined to save everybody else's. No living relative of Matt's was on speaking terms with him, but Tony still hadn't given up hope of somehow reconciling him with the rest of the clan. She refused to recognize the subtle hints of the futility of this mission, like Matt changing his last name or the fact that he hadn't attended his mother's funeral. "If Nora wants to speak to me, I'm sure she can find me."

"She probably thinks the exact same thing," Tony said, placing her empty cup in the dishwasher.

"Give it a rest, Tony. It's not something you can fix with good intentions and two minutes of fraternal chatter over the commlink."

She made a face but didn't press it further. "Fine, I won't mention Nora again. Just make sure I'll have my decadent cruise vacation."

Matt threw his hands up.

"If that's all it takes, you'll have it. In fact, I'm off to make sure it happens." He stood up. "Wish me luck. Something tells me it's going to be an interesting run."

Chapter Two

The bridge was surprisingly roomy for a spaceship this size. Together with the sensor array, it took up the entire bow, and its window screen gave a nice panoramic view. Right now it was fitted for a pilot and a copilot/navigator, though Matt had never had one of those, preferring to rely on his own abilities and the ship's computer.

Faine was already waiting for him there, looking slightly bored as he stood examining the control panel. Really, it was kind of ridiculous how gorgeous he was, even with the austere attire and the buzz cut that made his blond hair look darker than it was. It would have been unfair for anybody to have such perfect looks, but thankfully Faine made up for it with what Matt had already judged to be a stuffed-shirt personality.

"I see you're making yourself familiar with the place," Matt said, leaning on the back of the pilot's chair. It took a conscious effort not to automatically occupy it, but he had to at least try to make a welcoming impression. As much as it grated on his nerves, Faine was in charge as far as this job was concerned, since the twenty-thousand advance was already safely deposited in Matt's account. "Go ahead, see how it feels."

Faine climbed into the seat and ran his hands over the control panel, lighting it up. Then he touched his adapter implants, creating a link with the ship's computer. The huge canopy window darkened and the ship's schematics and technical specs came onto the resulting screen.

"Ah," he said after a few moments of inspecting the blueprints. "That's nice. Did you do the engine upgrade yourself?"

Matt beamed at the praise. It was his baby, after all. Always nice when she was appreciated.

"Me and Val. Well, Val does most of the actual work down there; I participate in the design and the testing." And the financing, damn it. And not like Val let anyone really help out in the engine room; he was convinced they'd do it all wrong.

"So, where are we going, and why couldn't I do it?" He let go of the pilot's chair and slumped onto the second seat, trying to get comfortable.

"There." A star map appeared on-screen, and with a touch, Faine zoomed in on a distant solar system. It had three planets revolving around a red sun, one of them separated from the rest by what looked to be a narrow asteroid field.

"The Colanta system. My employer has reasons to believe the Mnirians had some sort of a base there. More specifically, on one of the moons of Colanta-3." He pointed to the rather large isolated planet behind the belt. "I'm sure I don't have to tell you how rare and valuable Mnirian artifacts are."

Matt whistled softly. The Mnirians were an ancient alien civilization, now presumably extinct. The traces of their expansion spanned the reaches of the known galaxy. In fact, deep-space travel was possible only due to the network of enormous jumpgates they had left behind in almost every solar system, including the one found between the rings of Saturn. When activated by a sequence of laser pulses, the jumpgates generated a wormhole, connecting two sequence-specific points in space and time. Almost any ship equipped with a computer for precise coordinate calculations and a high-energy laser array needed for the activation could perform the jump through any existing gate. It was a testament to the Mnirian ingenuity that the millennia-old technology that made this possible had not yet been successfully replicated by any of the known spacefaring civilizations.

Mnirian structures and artifacts were few and far between. Finding a previously unknown Mnirian site that wasn't under Federation military or alien control was like tapping a veritable gold mine, since black market prices for such relics were astronomical. But their trade was highly illegal. No wonder Mr. Ari had been so evasive. It made Matt wary too, not only of the possible entanglement with the law, but of his client and his agent as well.

"Hard to believe nobody had found it before. But considering the location… Yeah. And is your employer looking for a specific artifact, or does he just want to clean the joint?"

"It's a specific item," Faine said. "But the particulars aren't important now. In fact, it isn't something you should concern yourself with at all, Captain. Your job is merely providing the vessel and getting us through any Federal control points along the way."

"It's good to be needed," Matt said. "And where exactly do you come in on the job?"

"Here," Faine continued, pointing at the asteroid field. "This is the real challenge in getting there. We still don't know what it is, exactly—real asteroids, debris from some ancient explosion, or an artificial safeguard placed there to protect the base. Either way, we will have to navigate it in order to land on the moon."

"That's impossible," Matt said, frowning as he examined the map. "*Lady Lisa* is fast and compact, but she's not built for that kind of maneuvering."

"We'll need something smaller, like your landing shuttle."

"Even with a shuttle, it would be extremely difficult. The shuttle is mostly manually operated. You'd have to have Falcon fighter training to fly it through that belt, especially if it's rigged by an alien species."

"I can do it," Faine said coolly. "I was hired for a reason."

Matt gave him a look. In all his life, he'd known only a handful of people who were capable of doing what Faine was proposing. He looked too young to have had that sort of practice, but his employer wanted him specifically for such a dubious task, replacing someone who had years of experience and reputation... The bad feeling Matt had gotten earlier intensified.

"You know those shiny toys can't do the work for you," he said, gesturing at Faine's adapters.

The other man drew back.

"They're good enough," he said curtly. "I'm good enough. We're wasting time. When can we take off?"

Matt was sorely tempted to tell him off. Yes, he could hardly ask for credentials in his line of work, but that didn't mean he was comfortable risking his crew's safety on the say-so of some self-proclaimed hotshot. But Val wanted his air compressor, and Tony wanted her vacation, and for them both to get their long-deserved wishes, he had to first get the money. So he swallowed everything he wanted to tell Faine, along with his pride, and said:

"We're waiting on Val. He should be here any moment. Once he's on board and gives us the go-ahead, feel free to take her for a spin."

☆☆☆

Fifteen minutes later, Matt was watching the intercom monitor as Val drove a service forklift loaded with compressor and pump parts up the ramp to the main hatch. It all looked like old junk to him, but no doubt

Val saw it as a potential treasure trove. He really was a tech wizard, though it was difficult to tell at first glance.

Big, heavy-muscled, and taciturn, most people automatically placed Val in the brawn rather than brain category. Highlights from his criminal record did nothing to dissipate that impression. On the other hand, Matt knew him as a talented engineer with a passion for nineteenth-century Russian literature, which he had once explained was his way of connecting with his cultural roots.

There were no produce packets among the items on the forklift, and that meant Tony was bound to be disappointed.

This entire time, Faine had been quietly running the ship's schematics on-screen. As soon as Val was safely inside with his catch, Matt called him to the bridge.

Faine glanced up warily as the engineer entered, carrying a midsized metal crate full of electronics under his arm. He gave Faine a once-over, nodded a silent greeting, and turned to Matt.

"This is Mr. Faine," Matt said. "He represents our client and will be piloting the *Lisa* to destination."

"Huh," was all Val said, but it didn't sound optimistic. Faine's cheeks colored slightly.

"How soon can we take off?" Matt asked, before things had the chance to escalate into unpleasantness.

Val shrugged. Even if he had reservations about Faine's presence, he would never question the captain's authority in front of strangers. In fact, unlike Tony, he rarely argued with Matt at all. "All the standard maintenance checkups are done. She's ready to go when you are."

"Good," Faine said dryly. "Then I propose we go now."

Matt and Val exchanged a look. Matt reminded himself once again of the advance he'd already accepted.

"Tell Tony we're leaving, will you?" he said to Val, and then turned to the pilot. "Take her out."

Faine nodded curtly and requested permission to take off from station control. *Lady Lisa* lifted slowly to the low hum of the auxiliary thrusters and glided majestically out of the dock bay doors into the starlit black.

The view never failed to take Matt's breath away, even after all these years. There was nothing like the feeling of utter insignificance when staring into that endless void. Some found it unsettling, but he found it peaceful. The cliché about how petty and trifling your troubles seemed when compared to the vastness of the universe was true, and there was a kind of serenity in that. Of course, that didn't go as far as saying he didn't care for his own insignificant existence while traversing said vastness. For instance, he was entirely unconvinced of the validity of Faine's plan to stomp through a potential obstacle course. Still, the scope of the risk was hard to gauge at this time. They would have to examine it more closely once they reached their final destination.

Matt watched as Faine's long fingers darted over the control panel. It was strange, sitting in what felt like a passenger seat of his own ship, just waiting to see what course she would take. The route details ran across the window screen for his benefit as the *Lisa* rounded the ungainly structure of the station. They were headed toward the outer rim of the Sonora system, where Freeport 16 orbited the red-and-purple gas planet of Sonora-7. The entire journey would take about five days—an ordinary run for *Lady Lisa* since they'd moved their base of operations to Sonora. Of course, once they made the jump from the Freeport gate they would be hundreds of light-years away.

"So, where are you from?" Matt asked, once they were safely outside the flow of the station's incoming and outgoing traffic. He hated to admit it, but he kind of liked Faine's calm and sure steering. No juvenile mad dashes to prove his superiority, no unnecessary movements.

"I grew up on Shyr-5," Faine said. "It's a small mining colony. Mostly iron and aluminum."

That was a peculiar choice of words. "Grew up" as in not born there? Faine didn't seem particularly forthcoming, but Matt wasn't about to let that discourage him.

"And what do you do for fun when you're not contracted by shady characters to illegally obtain priceless relics?"

Faine shot him a look.

"I study," he said with such seriousness that it threw Matt off for a second.

"Okay," he said slowly. "What is it you study?"

"Whatever I can. Math, physics, history."

Matt didn't know exactly how to respond to that, but he remembered Tony's suggestions regarding fun and plowed bravely on.

"You know, I could offer you tutorship in an additional subject," he said, "if you'd like to visit my cabin sometime while the autopilot is on.

No theory, pure practice, lots of recreation for everyone involved." He winked.

Faine looked at him with some confusion. He had long dark eyelashes, like a girl's.

"What?"

Okay, not so brilliant after all. "See, that's what happens when one does nothing but pilot and study," Matt said. "All work and no play, and all that. I was not too subtly inviting you to—"

"I got that," Faine interjected dryly. "What makes you think I would be interested?"

"Oh, I don't know, my irresistible appeal and good looks? A chance to unwind and have a good time on an otherwise boring trip to Freeport? Take your pick."

"I understand it would be too much to ask you to please go away, but may we at least change the topic of the conversation?" Faine said with a touch of exasperation.

Matt shrugged. It wasn't as if he really expected Faine to pounce on the offer. He was testing the waters, so to speak, and they were icy cold.

"You can't blame a guy for taking a shot," he said easily, stretching in his chair. "But it's my bloody ship, and I'm not going anywhere."

The screen went black, and a series of complex equations started to scroll down on it.

"You're not scaring me," Matt said dubiously.

"I like to spend my free time productively," Faine said. "You don't mind, do you?"

"You know, I'm gonna get some coffee," Matt said as he stood up. He needed a break anyway. "Feel free to have some once you're done with—" He waved vaguely at the screen. "—studying."

There was no information on the web on one Ryce Faine, but Matt expected as much. Having established that, he searched for Shyr-5, which turned out to be an iron-mining colony in the Sayler sector. His cabin computer provided pictures of utilitarian dome structures on a desolate, rocky landscape. The colony didn't offer much in terms of career opportunities other than flying those mining company freight barges Faine had mentioned earlier, and that was before it had been almost completely razed by an Alraki attack three years ago. The remaining survivors were making efforts to rebuild with government and commercial funding, but the prospects didn't look promising. None of the available positions would pose much of a challenge for the class of pilot Faine was claiming to be. If Faine was telling the truth about where he grew up, there was no way he could have acquired his training there. He certainly couldn't have afforded those top-notch new adapters.

Matt leaned back in his desk chair, frowning. He harbored a nagging suspicion about the man currently hogging his seat on the bridge, but it was so intangible that he decided to keep it to himself. Hopefully it wouldn't be coming around to bite him in the ass later.

He hadn't checked the bridge since they'd left the maintenance station yesterday, since he was in no mood for being around the other pilot. He wandered the ship aimlessly for a while, unnecessarily checking inventory and looking for things to do, until he found his crew members in the recreation room, watching a movie. When a run was going smoothly, the biggest problem aboard ship was boredom. It was a challenge not to go stir-crazy, with not much to do and nothing to differentiate between day and night aside from artificial lighting. That's why the rec room and the dining nook in the galley became the life centers for the crew, even when most of the time it was only the three of them.

Tony was sprawled in an oversized armchair, her eyes glued to the screen, while Val seemed immersed in an antique paper book. He had quite an extensive, if not very valuable, collection that consisted mostly of moldy classics, mystery novels, and pulp science fiction. Matt didn't share his fondness for old printed paper, though his entire childhood had been spent in a house full of precious antiques and rare tomes by famous authors ranging from the Romans to twenty-first-century philosophers. No pulp there.

There was a half-empty whiskey bottle and glasses on the side table, and Matt poured himself a drink.

"What's that you're reading?" he asked, motioning at the book with his chin.

"Turgenev. *The Diary of a Superfluous Man*," Val said in his deep, quiet voice, his eyes still glued to the page.

"I, personally, don't care for the classics," Matt declared. "All those people suffering prettily for no good reason make me sick."

"Prettily?" Val said, looking up. "Shows you don't know shit about Russian literature."

"'We can know only that we know nothing. And that is the highest degree of human wisdom,'" Matt quoted. "Tolstoy, I believe."

Val raised an eyebrow.

"Impressive," Tony remarked. "Who knew you'd retained some culture in you?"

Matt huffed dismissively. In truth, he didn't remember much else from the book apart from it being incredibly boring.

"How's it going up there?" Val asked, turning his attention back to the book.

"Oh, you know, everybody's still alive, so all in all, not bad," Matt said, sitting down on the old lounge sofa.

"That great, huh?"

"He's a pretentious snob," Matt said, sipping the whiskey. The amber liquid went down smoothly, bringing with it comforting warmth. "And I would know, I grew up around them."

"Meaning you struck out," Tony said with her usual shrewdness.

"I didn't strike out," Matt insisted. "I barely even came on to him. I'm merely giving him time alone to reflect on my dashing looks and animal magnetism."

Val snorted and turned another page.

"You won't get anywhere with this one," he said with disconcerting certainty.

"Yeah? How would you know?"

"I talked to him last night."

"You did?" Matt couldn't hide his astonishment. Val was not one for casual chitchat, and from what he'd seen of Faine, neither was he. "What did you two talk about?"

"He asked about the core engine upgrades," Val said. "And the new cooling system I installed. Showed me some diagrams he'd made for the auxiliary circuit override. He really knows his stuff."

That was the highest form of praise Val could bestow on anyone. Matt's eyebrows shot up.

"So?" he demanded defensively. "That doesn't mean anything."

"He's not your type," Val decreed with finality, turning his attention back to the book.

"Now, now," Tony said, coming to the rescue of Matt's wounded pride. "None of that defeatist talk. I bet the captain will get into this guy's pants by the time we make the jump from Freeport."

"That's the spirit!" Matt said, though deep down he was leaning toward agreeing with Val regarding his chances for success. "Place your bets, lady and gentleman."

"Hundred creds on the captain," Tony said.

"Fine," Val said, not looking up. "Good luck with that."

"Your vote of confidence is overwhelming," Matt said, getting up. He put down his glass but grabbed the bottle. "With those kinds of stakes, I'm gonna need all the help I can get. Your contribution to the cause won't be forgotten."

Tony saluted him and went back to watching the movie, while Val barely seemed to notice his exit.

Faine wasn't on the bridge, and the autopilot was on. Matt couldn't resist the urge to sit in the pilot's chair and connect to the controls, just to check on *Lisa*. The course for Freeport 16 was set, all systems were functional, and the engine was purring softly. The mere connection of mind and ship, the overall sense of control, was familiar and soothing. This was home, or as much of a home as he could ever hope to achieve.

He disconnected with a renewed sense of calm. Do the job, collect the pay, move on—that was what they did, and that was what they were going to do now, annoying upstart pilots notwithstanding.

Chapter Three

There were only so many places to go on a ship the size of *Lady Lisa*. Even so, Matt hadn't seen Faine around that much these past few days. He'd shown no inclination to mix with the crew in the rec room, fixed his meals on his own, and avoided using the gym. Matt, on his part, was reluctant to share the bridge with him again. In fact, he was reluctant to interact with Faine at all, but a bet was a bet, and time was running out. So on the evening of the third day of their journey, he headed for the only other place he could find him.

It took Faine a few moments to open his cabin door. He wore a gray sweat suit, and his cropped hair was still damp from a recent shower. Just this little detail kicked Matt's imagination into overdrive, and the image of Faine naked, with ionized water streaming over flawless pale skin, popped unbidden into his head. His mouth went a little dry.

"Yes, Captain?" Faine said, when the moment stretched into uncomfortable silence. "Did you want something?"

"Look, we got off on the wrong foot," Matt said, focusing on the task at hand and brandishing the bottle of whiskey like a peace offering. "How about we start over? Have a little chat, maybe a few drinks?"

For a moment, Matt thought Faine was going to decline, but he stepped back, letting Matt inside the cabin. Faine had unpacked his belongings, few as they were. His commlink was set on the foldout table, and his clothes were folded neatly on the shelves. Between the two of them, the small space felt crowded.

Matt sat down on the bunk bed.

"Why don't you get us a couple of glasses?" he said. "There should be some in the upper cupboard."

Faine hesitated for a second, but got two tumblers and settled down on a chair rather than share the bed next to Matt.

Matt poured whiskey into the tumblers and raised his in a salute.

"To a successful job," he said.

Faine nodded and took a sip, immediately making a face.

"That's…strong," he observed.

"It's not the most expensive stuff, but it gets the job done," Matt said, making himself more comfortable on the narrow bed. "So, you've had time to look at *Lisa*. What do you think?"

"She doesn't look like much at first glance," Faine said. "Phaeton vessels are robust and lack finesse. But the system overhaul you did on her is very impressive—like a whole new ship. It must have taken a lot of time."

Matt nodded, deciding that perhaps Faine did have redeeming qualities after all, apart from his looks.

"A lot of time and a lot of money. But it does give you that extra edge, you know. I wasn't lying when I said she's the fastest ship in the sector."

"I'm sure it's very important in your line of work," Faine said politely. His second shot seemed to go down more smoothly.

"It's important in everybody's line of work," Matt said. "Including yours, whatever it may be." He gestured at Faine with the glass. "I mean, why all the secrecy? I don't even know your real name. At least tell me what got you the hotshot reputation that made Mr. Ari hire you for the job. It certainly wasn't piloting freight barges on Shyr-5."

"Forgive me if I don't satisfy your curiosity, Captain. Sometimes, the more you know, the greater the danger." Faine smiled. "Besides, you're the kind of man who sells information. Not exactly someone to inspire trust."

"I'm the kind of man who sells everything," said Matt lightly. "But I rarely meet people who interest me personally."

"And I do?"

Faine really wasn't used to drinking the heavy stuff. He was slightly slumped in his chair, and was staring at the tumbler in his hand with intense focus. This was definitely playing into Matt's hands.

"Well, yeah," Matt said. "A handsome, mysterious stranger, working for a mysterious employer to retrieve a mysterious object from a place it's impossible to get to? Anyone would be intrigued."

Faine rolled his eyes and took another sip.

"I'm not stupid. I realize perfectly well why you're here, being nice and trying to get me drunk. I'm sorry to say you're barking up the wrong tree. I'm simply not interested; is that so hard to understand?"

"A little," Matt said, chagrined but unwilling to admit defeat just yet. What he was doing wasn't anywhere near proper, but the alcohol had made him bolder, and besides, Faine could tell him to fuck off if he wanted to. Right? "We're both adults and reasonably good-looking. What's wrong with having a little fun together? It's not like you're a blushing virgin."

Faine raised his head and looked at him sharply.

"Oh, my God," Matt said slowly. "You *are* a virgin."

His palms got sweaty, and his heart beat faster with the exhilaration of a hunter. That would be quite a feat, wouldn't it, to seduce the chaste ice prince? Granted, it was a long shot, and they had rather limited time, but it would boost Matt's self-confidence, not that it really needed boosting. Not to mention proving Val wrong.

"I'm half-Onorean," Faine said, a little defensively, rousing Matt from his optimistic reverie. "From what I understand, they don't consider an overdeveloped sex drive a desirable trait."

"What?" Matt said, frowning. "How can you be *half*-Onorean?"

A secluded independent colony, Onor specialized in advanced nanotechnologies and genomics. They believed in excluding any indetermination from the procreation process, opting instead to genetically engineer their offspring to have what they considered to be preferable attributes, like high intelligence and physical prowess. There were some who questioned whether the Onoreans were even human anymore, or whether they had transcended into a whole new species. But since they were a very closed community, which very rarely allowed incomers, the point was somewhat moot. Though many Onoreans ventured abroad for business and research purposes, it was unheard of for one to leave the colony permanently, or marry an outsider.

Faine pursed his lips. It was probably more than he had wanted to reveal, but it was too late to back down now.

"My mother was Onorean," he said grudgingly. "She was on an off-world research expedition when they were waylaid by pirates. I don't know why she chose to give birth to her rapist's baby, but she did, and she put me out for adoption. That's how I ended up in the Shyr colony. My adoptive parents raised me since I was five months old."

There was an awkward silence while Matt took that in. It certainly explained a lot of things, like Faine's chiseled features, his intelligence, and his air of aloof superiority. And yes, the reduced interest in the kind of recreational activities Matt had been suggesting. He didn't quite know what to say now, and the liquor wasn't really helping. Faine's story reminded him of his own unfortunate run-in with pirates, and it really wasn't something he cared to dwell on.

Space piracy wasn't uncommon, especially in the more "rural" sectors, where the Federal military presence was incidental. Most of these pirates were no more than gangs operating on way stations and trading posts, but some were armed and equipped enough to actually take over entire ships, successfully evading Federation raids. Matt had the misfortune to have encountered one of these pirate vessels during his brief stint as a navigator for the North Star drilling company, operating in the sparsely populated Lea system. He still had nightmares about that incident.

Faine gulped down the rest of his drink and grimaced.

"Regardless of my inclinations, I don't fraternize with criminals," he said. His speech was already a little slurred.

"Excuse me?" Matt was a little thrown off balance by that statement. It was true he wasn't exactly the most law-abiding citizen, but he didn't think of himself as a hardened criminal either.

"You think I don't know about the twenty crates of contraband Earth-grown coffee you have in the cargo hold right now, marked and declared as soluble fiber dye?"

"Really, that's..."

"Yes, it's just coffee. But those are still smuggled goods, and that's what you do. You carry black market contraband and illegal passengers. Otherwise, you wouldn't have taken this job and let some stranger pilot your ship. You have no qualms about breaking the law for money, when it suits you. You faulted me for not giving my real name, yet yours is an alias as well, *Mr. Spears.*"

He took the bottle and poured himself another drink. His movements were slow and a bit too precise, but his hands were steady.

"And your crew is no better," he continued. "I've accessed the ship records; I've read their personal files. Your engineer, Valeriy Sokolov, served five years in a high-security correctional facility for aggravated assault and attempted murder. And your first mate, Antonia Joyce, was accused of embezzlement and theft of prescription medication and fired from the Interstellar Medical Aid network where she worked as a trial coordinator to become, basically, a mercenary. Are you really going to try to convince me you're anything more than a bunch of felons, trying to scrape by using whatever means necessary?"

As if the little pup knew shit.

"Look, kid," Matt said. He kept his voice calm and made a conscious effort not to clench his fists. Pretty face or not, now he was really tempted to punch it. "I don't care who you are or who you're working for, or how much he's paying. You don't talk about my crew like that. Their past is none of your business. My past is way beyond your business. Sometimes people do what they have to do, and nobody asked you to pass judgment. Besides, for somebody sitting on that mighty high horse, you sure look a lot like a mercenary yourself."

For a few tense moments, they stared at each other with varying degrees of resentment. Finally Faine looked away, rubbing his forehead with the heel of his palm.

"I'm gonna let that slide because you're wasted," Matt said, getting up. "And because technically you represent my client."

"That didn't hinder you from trying to ply me with alcohol to get me in bed," Faine retorted snappishly. "Hardly what one could call professional behavior."

"Oh for God's sake," Matt said disgustedly. "You make it sound as if I tried to drug you and have my wicked way with you. Lighten up and go easy on the drama, will you? Nobody was threatening your precious virtue. I might be a criminal to you, but I can take a 'no.'"

Faine stared moodily at his glass and said nothing, which Matt took as his cue to leave, grabbing the bottle and heading out, wishing he could pointedly slam the door behind him.

☆☆☆

He was cold. That was always the first thing he remembered—lying half-naked on the cold sticky floor, slowly regaining consciousness. A strong metallic taste lingered in his mouth. Pushing up on one elbow, his head throbbed dully, and pain radiated behind his eyes. When he pressed a shaking hand to his forehead, his fingers came away smeared with blood. Pieces of memory were coming back to him, and bile rose up in his throat. He looked around wildly, searching for a way out, but the compartment was little more than a cargo storage locker.

A faint greenish glow illuminated the room, empty save for two or three rusty crates in the corner. The stench of untended mold vied with the smell of his fear and stale sweat. Where were the others? Were they all dead?

Heavy footsteps resonated from the outside corridor. He flinched as the door opened with a rusty screech, the fluorescent light pouring in and almost blinding him. Voices boomed in the tiny room, laughing, cursing. The men's faces were distorted, his mind shying away from detail. They hauled him up and shoved him into the corridor. He slipped and fell, sprawling on the floor, and a heavy boot caught him in the stomach. He tried to curl into a ball, but they lifted him up again, and he was dragged on. He couldn't make out how many were there, or how long the corridor was, or the layout of the ship. Just the thick, cloying fear. He was going to die, and it wasn't going to be quick.

The dream fragmented at this point. One minute he was being dragged down the long corridor, the next he was already hanging by his wrists, stripped to the waist. And then he was back in it, full force. There was laughter and jeering as he struggled in the bonds.

"Who's this little shit?" a deep voice said. Someone grabbed his face and jerked his head roughly back.

Dylan Rodgers. He'd know that voice anywhere.

Wake up. You know what's going to happen. Wake up.

"He's the company navigator," someone said behind him.

"Yes, I see," Rodgers said. Matt blinked rapidly, focusing on the reflection of his face in the knife blade the man was holding. An old-fashioned steel knife, not an electric one. "The one who led us a fucking chase. Looks like we got ourselves a troublemaker here. How about we make sure he won't be flying no more, boys?"

No, please, no.

His head was filled with shrieking, but in the dream he was mute, powerless to stop the blade that sliced at his adapters, tearing skin, nerve, and microscopic wiring. Pain blossomed, vicious and glaringly bright, erupting like fireworks.

The dream shattered.

Matt opened his eyes, staring blindly into the darkness, heart pounding. His T-shirt was drenched in sweat. He sat up and gingerly touched the adapters on his temples to reassure himself they were still there. His throat felt dry, as if he had hurt it screaming.

He rubbed his face in a futile attempt to erase the last dregs of the nightmare. Fuck Faine for bringing up pirates, and fuck that bastard Rodgers for pulling that shit on him. He hadn't had one of those dreams in months, and now it all came flooding back.

But it was a dream, nothing more. He was safe here, on his own ship, in this sector. Sure, there were bad people out there, but thankfully the Federation presence was too prominent in Sonora for the pirates' liking. They preferred easier, more remote targets, like deep-space cargo vessels with no military convoy. It was all that reminiscing that had conjured up the dream, nothing more. But despite repeating it over and over to himself, he didn't go back to sleep.

☆☆☆

The smell of Tony's cooking did nothing for Matt's hangover.

After waking up from the nightmare, he'd spent the rest of the night in his cabin with the remainder of the whiskey to keep him company. In retrospect, his behavior showed a slip in wisdom and decorum, but hitting on the pilot and then getting drunk off his ass wasn't the first mistake he'd made in the last few days. As far as he was concerned, anyone with an opinion could chalk it all up to his disreputable reputation, and shove it.

"Coffee," he moaned as he dragged himself into the galley and eased carefully into a seat at the table. He buried his head in his hands, shielding his eyes from the glare of glossy white tabletop under the bright fluorescent lighting.

"My, what a lovely shade of green you are," Tony said as she turned on the coffee machine and sat down to finish her breakfast. At least the sound of percolating brew was soothing.

"I take it your long-anticipated date didn't go well?" she continued after a bit.

"It wasn't a date. We just got drunk and insulted each other."

"Sounds like most of your dates." She shrugged and got up to rinse her dishes.

"At least I get laid on most of my dates. If I wanted to be scolded and thrown out, I'd go visit my father," he said sourly.

Tony placed a large mug of steaming coffee in front of him, and Matt took it gratefully. The first bitter sip, though scalding hot, made him a little more at peace with the world.

"Sorry, Tony, it looks like you're gonna lose those hundred creds. Doesn't it grate on your nerves how Val is always right about these things? I mean, what does he know? He was married for like fifteen years. This is the last time I'm endorsing gambling on whether or not I can get into somebody's pants."

"Ahem," Tony said in a different voice.

Oh shit.

"Hey, Ryce," Tony was saying as she moved to busily put away her plate and mug, while Matt stared at his mug, wishing he could disappear into it. "Would you like some coffee?"

If he asks whether it's contraband, I'm going to punch him in the face, Matt thought dully. Thankfully, Faine—Ryce—was apparently in worse shape than him and didn't question the origins of whatever would make him feel better at the moment.

"Yes, thank you," Ryce said gratefully as he sat across from Matt. His eyes were red-rimmed. Tony dispensed him a cup of coffee and left, throwing Matt a look laden with significance.

"How much did you hear?" Matt said, once she was safely out of earshot.

Ryce shrugged. He gazed into his cup as if it held the secrets of the universe, and then sighed.

"I can't say I'm surprised," he said. "Though I must admit I didn't expect actual betting to take place."

They sat for a while in uncomfortable silence. Matt was expecting a confrontation, but Ryce seemed to forgo his usual cocky attitude. If anything, he looked despondent, and it wasn't as satisfying a sight as Matt would have expected.

He rubbed his forehead wearily. "If it helps any, I wasn't doing the betting. The guys were just having fun; it wasn't personal. But it wasn't in good taste, and it wasn't the right thing to do. For what it's worth, I'm sorry I came on to you like I did. I behaved like an asshole, and you didn't deserve that."

Ryce only nodded. He drank his brew slowly, avoiding eye contact, and then said, somewhat reluctantly:

"I believe I was a bit out of line too. You're right; I shouldn't have read your crew's records. At the very least I shouldn't have said anything about them."

"Tony and Val are good people," Matt said, somewhat mollified. "Everybody makes wrong decisions sometimes, or gets knocked down. I'm sure even you've made some mistakes in your life. And if you haven't, you will. And then you'll want someone to give you a second chance too. That's kinda our thing here on the *Lisa*, see. Each one of us needed a second chance after making a complete mess of their lives. Granted, it's not much of an opportunity, but we got each other's backs. And I, for one, don't care if my first mate stole some drugs on her previous job to help some poor sod who couldn't afford them, or if my engineer did hard time because he punched the shit out of the guy who raped his wife. As long as they're straight with me, we're good."

"It wasn't really about them," Ryce admitted. "I didn't come here expecting to find a congregation of saints. But I don't like being treated like a diversion."

"Again, sorry about that," Matt said. "But you have to admit, you've been a little standoffish."

"I apologize. I've felt like a circus freak all my life, and I hate it when people come on to me for the novelty. It's not that I'm averse to the idea of having a physical relationship at some point; I just haven't met anybody that interests me that way, and people usually have a hard time accepting that." He swooshed the dregs of his coffee, looking into the mug pensively.

That sounded about right. Wasn't Matt himself intrigued by the thought of being the one to thaw him out? His Onorean background indicating that he was probably borderline genius added more thrill into the mix. For all his haughtiness, there was an edge of insecurity to Ryce's demeanor, a sense of not belonging. That was something Matt could definitely relate to.

"You know what?" he said, getting up to refill their mugs. He was feeling marginally better about himself, and his headache seemed to be clearing. "Let's just forget about it and focus on the job at hand. I promise I won't make a move on you again. Unless you'd want me to, of course, and tell me so." He winked at Ryce.

"I'll drink to that." Rice smiled back at him. His gaze flicked between the door and Matt. "Wouldn't she be upset at you for doing that, though?"

"Who, Tony? Why would she be upset?"

"She seems very fond of you," Ryce said carefully.

"Hey, it's not like that. She's not interested in me that way. Besides, I don't shit where I eat."

Ryce arched an eyebrow. "Really? I feel I should be offended somehow."

"It's different. You're not a part of the team." Matt shrugged. "It's a onetime gig, and then we won't see each other again."

Ryce smirked and got up, taking his mug with him. "I think that would be wise." He paused at the doorway as if about to say something else and then shook his head and saluted Matt with the mug.

Before Matt had a chance to respond, the alarm lights flashed red, and the ship computer announced: "Unidentified spacecraft approaching. Repeat, unidentified spacecraft approaching."

Chapter Four

Ryce and Matt exchanged worried looks and hurried to the bridge. There was an awkward shuffle as both of them reached for the pilot seat. Matt threw his hands up and took the other chair. He itched to take over—he was the captain and it was his responsibility, and he didn't trust the kid to know what he was doing. But a deal was a deal, and he promised himself he could always reconnect and override the pilot's controls if it became necessary.

Ryce nodded in acknowledgment of his concession and connected to the console. The image of the unknown ship came up on-screen, 100 klicks away but clearly discernible.

"Shit," Matt said, his heart sinking. Ryce said nothing, switching to manual and taking hold of the control stick.

"What the hell are they doing here?" Matt said, still having difficulty believing his eyes. It felt unreal, like a bad dream. It couldn't be happening. "Sonora is in the middle of Federation space! There are at least four Fleet stations in the system."

"Well, there aren't any Fleet vessels here right now," Ryce said, his attention focused on the screen. "Nothing within hailing distance. I'm sending out a distress signal in case anybody is close enough to hear."

Matt cursed and flipped on the voice communication system.

"This is the bridge. We have encountered an Alraki vessel. Be on alert and strap up." It wouldn't be of much help if they were boarded, but at least Tony and Val would know what to expect.

The alien ship was approaching fast, making no attempt to hail them. For them, there was no need. The Alraki had no treaties with the Federation and honored no existing conventions. They were vultures and scavengers, in a state of perpetual war with the humans, as well as with half a dozen other alien species, most notably the Parveni and the Drodezians, who were nominally allied with the Federation. It was a flow of endless skirmishes, while the Alraki preyed on isolated colonies and outposts situated too far out to receive immediate backup.

Standing at over seven feet tall and half as wide, the Alraki were creatures of nightmares. They were vaguely humanoid if you ignored the two extra extremities and claws so sharp they could eviscerate a human with one stroke. So integrated were their bodies and armor that it was difficult to tell which was which. Matt had seen them up close and personal a few times, and he wasn't ready for a chance to meet them again. Certainly not when it was ship against ship in open space. *Lady Lisa* was a cargo vessel and not equipped to engage in battles. Installing weapons systems on haulers, such as a Phaeton, was prohibited under Federal law, and Matt had never tampered with that sort of thing for fear of losing his flight license. Of course, that seemed like a trifle when suddenly faced with a hostile warship.

Ryce turned the ship around in a swift fluid motion, speeding away, but there wasn't a lot he could do or anywhere he could go. The Alraki were gaining on them even though *Lady Lisa* was going nearly full throttle. The computer beeped in alarm, and the entire ship shook as a blast of light exploded on-screen.

"Fuck! They're firing torpedoes at us!" Matt said in what was probably the epitome of stating the obvious. His heart was thundering louder than the sound of the alarm. He tapped on the console, looking for signs of damage, but thankfully they didn't seem to have sustained a direct hit. Yet.

"EM pulse torpedoes. They're aiming to shut down the engines and the computer, take us up and gut the ship." Damn it, why wasn't anyone responding to their signal? He often complained there was a Federation cruiser within spitting distance at any point in Sonora, so where were they when you needed one?

"Not your first Alraki battleship, I take it?" Ryce said. He looked much too calm. There was another blast, but *Lady Lisa* slewed abruptly to the right to avoid the projectile a fraction of a second before impact. Matt drew a sharp breath. Their luck was going to run out very soon.

"I know enough to realize we're screwed. We're an easy target, and they know it." Matt ran the options in his head, but they were rather limited. Their chances for escape were almost nonexistent. The enemy was already too close. Their ship was a smaller frigate, not a cruiser, and carried no fighters aboard, relying instead on speed and firepower. They couldn't abandon the *Lisa*; the Alraki would shoot down a much slower shuttle in a matter of seconds. And staying on board meant they would have to engage in hand-to-hand combat with the Alraki. Given there were only the four of them, they would be at a serious disadvantage, especially if the artificial gravity and auxiliary systems were paralyzed with an EM blast. Either way, their prospects didn't appear cheerful.

"Didn't you brag that this was the fastest ship in the sector?" Ryce inquired.

"It is, but we can't outrun them when they're shooting EMs at us! One hit and we're adrift belly up, waiting to be boarded."

"Then we don't let them hit us. Hold on," Ryce said, and *Lady Lisa* surged forward and up, barely avoiding another torpedo. The fact they were still up in the air was nothing short of astonishing, and this waste of ammunition was bound to make the Alraki angry. They definitely wouldn't just give up the chase.

Ryce made a quick turn about without slowing down. Everything on the bridge that wasn't nailed to the floor shuffled and bumped into walls. Matt grabbed the armrests and fervently hoped Tony and Val had the sense to heed his order to strap themselves up. Meanwhile, *Lady Lisa* sped toward the enemy ship with the determination of a kamikaze flier on a collision course.

"What are you doing?" The Alraki ship was now closer than Matt ever wanted to be to an enemy vessel without a Fleet cruiser somewhere nearby, preferably between them.

"They won't be able to fire the EMs once we're close enough," Ryce said. "They'd risk incapacitating themselves."

"I'm sure they have trusty laser guns they can use!" Matt's heart sank as he remembered the cargo. It should have been okay in the hold, but with the EM torpedoes, the prospective laser hits, and Ryce apparently dogfighting the Alraki vessel, things could potentially turn ugly. "Shit. If they hit us with those, we're toast. We have volatile cargo." He really didn't want to admit this, but it was better if Ryce fully understood the gravity of the situation before he decided to play "chicken" with the aliens.

Ryce raised an eyebrow. "Since when is coffee volatile?"

"It's not coffee! Well, not all of it. I have a few barrels of PETN on board. It's stabilized, but the stabilizers won't hold if we crash into that thing."

Ryce threw him a hard look. "Why are you carrying pentaerythritol tetranitrate?"

"Look," Matt said. "I'm really impressed you can even pronounce that, but does it really matter why I have it? It's here, and it's a fucking explosive, and if the Alraki fire at us with more than those EMs, there are gonna be pieces of us floating all over Sonora!"

"Fine," Ryce said curtly. The ship shook as it evaded another torpedo, but stayed true to course. "Actually, that may help."

Matt stared at him, but there really wasn't any time to wonder whether the man was crazy. The Alraki vessel was growing larger and larger on-screen. Matt had seen plenty of spaceships in his life, and they were all very distinct. Humans favored simple, utilitarian design, while other races ranged in preferences from bulky and geometric to fanciful and organic. The Alraki ships were too foreign, their shape oddly twisted and irregular to the human eye, like a scaly dragon coiling on itself. Very little was known of Alraki culture and way of life, but the bit that had filtered through appeared as strange as the outlines of their ships.

With *Lady Lisa* hurtling right at them, the Alraki gave up on the EMs but didn't initiate an evasive maneuver either, opting instead to use laser fire, as Matt had feared. Bright red beams tore the blackness, aiming for the ship's vulnerable points. Yet somehow, *Lady Lisa* managed to avoid the blasts, dodging them with surprising agility. For all her speed, she was a hauler, not a fighter, but right now she was maxing that engine for all it was worth and more. There was no way this was luck, and there was no way Ryce had learned to maneuver like this on a freight barge. This was high-level training.

A proximity warning notice flashed red on-screen. They were too close to the other ship, and coming closer with every second. Matt could distinguish what looked like portholes and hatches on the sides of the Alraki battleship.

"They won't budge!" he warned.

"That's what I'm counting on."

There was no way in hell Matt was going to let this crazy bastard destroy his ship and kill them all. He cursed and reached for his adapters, but before he could activate the connection, Ryce pulled the control stick sharply. The ship soared, cutting over the Alraki vessel and skimming close by its hull. Matt sucked in his breath as they flew over the spiky sail, going up and up in a dizzying zoom. Bile rose in his throat at the sudden near miss on occupying the same point in space as the other ship.

Across the view screen, a warning notice streamed in angry red script: *Cargo bay doors open. Warning. Cargo bay doors open. Emergency release.*

"No!" Matt cried. But it was already too late. In his mind's eye he saw the heavy bottom hatch sliding open. He tapped at the console frantically, bringing up the feed from the bottom view cameras, just in time to watch as their entire cargo dropped into space, sucked out of the open doors by the vacuum, the containers and the barrels scattering beneath them.

It was as if his seat had been yanked out from under him, leaving him breathless and speechless. All he could do was stare at the tons of dangerous contraband floating like so much space debris around the hull of the alien ship.

"There we go," Ryce whispered.

Lady Lisa veered to the right, going full speed ahead. Matt's stomach lurched as the engines strained to their full capacity to speed the ship away. And just in time, as the next laser fired from the Alraki ship hit one of the spinning barrels.

The explosion was so bright they had to shield their eyes for a second. *Lady Lisa* shuddered again but stayed on course, as one explosion triggered another and then another, sending off volleys of shrapnel. The Alraki ship swiveled in a desperate attempt to evade the eruptions, but the initial explosion had torn into the hull near the top of the sail, and now it was burning. Bluish-white flames flared amid the spikes, going out almost instantly. The battleship continued its maneuver, pulling away from the detonating pieces.

"Fuck," Matt said quietly, mesmerized by the action unfurling on the rear view. The explosions finally subsided, the PETN having exhausted itself. It was one of the craziest things he had ever witnessed. "Let's hope they don't chase us."

"I think they might be too busy to worry about us now." Ryce was focused on running a systems check for signs of damage.

Matt could only sit and stare at him. How anyone could stay so calm through this kind of shit-storm was beyond him. Level-headed, collected—yes. But icy-calm? Ryce was either clinically insane or had balls of steel, or both. Maybe it was an Onorean thing, or maybe he was trained as a superassassin for covert ops. Who the hell knew. But it was definitely more than he'd expected of him.

"I can't believe you did that. That could have easily blown up in our faces if we weren't fast enough."

"Well, it worked." Ryce shrugged. "That's what counts."

"Fuckers." Matt lowered his head and rubbed his eyes. He couldn't resist connecting to the ship, just to make sure everything was all right. But Ryce really knew his stuff, it seemed. There was no serious damage to the ship, and they were hightailing it before the Alraki recovered. Matt was betting the aliens wouldn't give chase anyway. Hopefully, avoiding contact with any military vessels that might be called to the area would be a higher priority.

Thankfully, Ryce didn't say anything about the intrusion into the ship's controls.

"We're lucky they're not very persistent," he said, echoing Matt's thoughts. "They like sweeping in for an easy kill. A drawn-out battle is not their preferred tactic."

"That wasn't your first Alraki battleship either, huh?" Matt recalled that at the peak of the war, the Alraki had hit the mining colony where Ryce had grown up. Assuming, of course, he was telling the truth about his origins.

"No," Ryce said, pursing his lips. Complete diagnostics of the ship's systems appeared on-screen, more for Matt's benefit. "My adoptive parents were killed in a raid."

Before Matt could respond to that, Tony's terse voice said over the comm: "Permission to come on the bridge." Matt cringed, but pressed the door open.

Tony stepped inside, looking extremely unhappy. She threw Ryce a sidelong look and turned to Matt.

"What was that?" she asked.

"That was an Alraki ship trying to hijack us," Matt said, though he knew that was not what she meant. "And now we're getting the hell out of here before they decide to come after us. You've set the course to Freeport 16 again, right?" Matt asked Ryce.

"Yes, Captain," he said politely, seeming to ignore the tension in the room. "We've sustained a few glancing hits. There's only minor damage to the hull; I'm sure your engineer can fix that."

"And who's going to fix all those goods you just threw out the window?" Tony demanded angrily. "I nearly had a heart attack watching the external camera feed. Do you have any idea what you've done?"

Ryce opened his mouth, but Matt jumped out of his chair and ushered Tony into the corridor before he had a chance to respond and worsen the situation by being annoyingly right. She glared at him, but held her tongue long enough for them to reach the galley.

"What were you thinking?" she began, rounding on him.

"It saved our lives," he cut in, before she could build up steam. "There was no way we could get away from them. It wasn't my idea, and I didn't like it either, but we had no choice. In fact, I think it was kind of brilliant."

"Brilliant?" Tony sputtered. "Is that what you're going to tell Pat Gentry when he asks what happened to his goddamned cargo? Do you think he's going to care about the Alraki?"

It was a purely rhetorical question. Pat Gentry headed the black market and drug network on Sonora-7 and the neighboring stations and trading posts, including Freeport 16. While he was by no means a criminal mastermind, Gentry ran his operation with brutal efficiency, and for him, brutal meant exactly that. He would definitely not care about Matt's altercations with the Alraki, or with anyone else for that matter, but he would care about losing his precious and very illegal explosives.

They had picked up the PETN from a small underground manufacturing facility on one of the moons of Sonora-2. The deal was they would drop it off at Freeport, disguised as a shipment of soluble dye mixed in with the stock of contraband coffee they had purchased previously. Matt knew some people on the station, and for the right price, they wouldn't look too closely at his freights, though this was the first time he had tried to carry something so illicit. Tony wasn't happy about it when he took Gentry's offer, but they'd been running low on cash for a while, and Gentry had paid a hefty sum up front. Matt tried not to think too much about what he needed the explosives for. He'd learned not to ask questions and not to burden his conscience with things he couldn't change.

"Let me worry about Gentry," he said. "There's nothing we can do about the cargo now anyway. The important thing is we're still alive, and as much as it pains me to say it, it wasn't my doing." He lowered his voice. "I don't know what his deal is, but I've never seen anybody maneuver a Phaeton like that. I didn't know that was even possible."

If there was anything positive that had stuck with Matt from his days in the Fleet, it was respect for good old straightforward guts. He hadn't seen Ryce as someone who had it; he'd come off as snotty, and his youth spoke of inexperience. He'd never thought someone like that would keep his cool under pressure, and in such a spectacular way. It suddenly made him look at Ryce in a whole different light.

"I know. We felt it," Tony muttered. "He must have mistaken the *Lisa* for a Falcon fighter. Don't get me wrong, I'm glad he pulled us out of that situation, but it felt like we were going through a meat grinder. I can't believe the Alraki would venture so far into the sector! The Feds better get a grip on things."

"Yeah, like that would ever happen," Matt said. Tony's comment about a Falcon fighter had an unpleasant ring to it. The last thing Matt wanted was to get in the middle of anything that involved the military, however remotely.

Tony shook her head. "Gentry won't just let it slide, Matt. He's going to be mad as hell."

"I know. But it's all business, right?" Matt produced a fake smile, trying to sound confident and matter-of-fact. "Business partners can always reach a mutually beneficial agreement."

She looked unconvinced. It was annoying how she always saw through his bullshit. It made it difficult for him to believe it.

"I hope you're right. Because otherwise, the Alraki might have been the safer option."

Chapter Five

The round bulk of Freeport 16 filled the screen. The four corner installments of the Mnirian jumpgate, dark and etched in silver, were presently hidden from view behind its hull.

All Freeport stations were built similarly, with a massive outer ring that housed the common areas, hangars, guest accommodations and docks, and a small inner ring designated for station personnel. Freeports were originally established to regulate traffic through the Mnirian jumpgates to the more densely populated systems. Over time, they had become central hubs of transportation and commerce. This Freeport could harbor up to twenty thousand people at any given moment.

Traffic was thick and constant, and Matt had been waiting in orbit for half an hour for permission to dock. He was presently alone on the bridge. Since Ryce wasn't registered to the *Lisa* in any official capacity, it fell to Matt to communicate with station control and take the ship in.

Thankfully, the rest of the journey here had been uneventful, but the shore leave couldn't have come soon enough. It hadn't been a long run by any means, but the atmosphere aboard *Lady Lisa* following the Alraki attack was tense, and they all needed a break from each other, however brief. Matt wasn't planning on staying at Freeport long; they had to refuel, do a maintenance check, and pick up enough supplies to last them through the next run. Considering it was going to be a run with many unknown variables—like the poorly charted destination, a stand-alone jumpgate with no regulatory station, and a difficult flying route—Matt wanted to make sure they had more than enough fuel and that there wouldn't be any unpleasant surprises when it came to the ship's mechanics. He liked to be ready for every contingency.

He also had to contact Pat Gentry and tell him his cargo was lost; he wasn't looking forward to that at all. Stalling for a bit while he figured out the best way to handle this might be the way to go.

The first order of business after safe docking was scheduling a jump. Freeport 16 was an important hub, and its jumpgate operated at full capacity.

"Please state your destination," the pleasant computer voice said when he contacted jump control and gave his ship's registration number.

"Colanta system," Matt said. Thankfully it was still in Federation space, and so wouldn't require any special permits by the Foreign Office.

The computer processed his request.

"There is no Freeport station available in the Colanta system," it said at last. "Jump autoactivation technology is required for return journey. Is such equipment installed on your ship, and is it in working order?"

The station maintenance inspection crew would immediately retire any ship lacking such equipment anyway. With the Freeport network so widely spread through the galaxy, space travel rarely required a ship to autoactivate a jumpgate, but nobody wanted to find themselves stranded thousands of light-years away from civilization if something went wrong.

"Yes," he said.

"Please confirm destination: Colanta system," the computer reiterated.

"Confirmed," Matt said.

"Your jump to the Colanta system is scheduled for June 16, 18:30 standard Freeport Time," the computer announced. "Please make sure to enter the queue fifteen minutes before the appointed time. Failure to do so will result in cancellation of your departure and will curry fines."

"Sure," Matt said and disconnected. They had two days until the jump, which gave him plenty of time for all the arrangements and some well-deserved R & R. Thankfully, a station as big as the Freeport offered more than enough choices of entertainment. Matt wasn't original in his pursuit of distractions. As soon as *Lisa* was safely inside the landing dock and they cleared the customs inspection, he was headed for a bar.

Ryce stepped inside just as he was about to leave the bridge.

"Captain, may I speak with you?"

"Sure." Matt lowered himself back into his chair. He'd been sort of avoiding Ryce for the past two days, contenting himself with short visits to the bridge when the other man was sleeping or otherwise occupied, and Ryce seemed to welcome this state of affairs. They had barely spoken to each other after the altercation with the Alraki. Matt had had a lot of time to turn things over in his head since then, and he didn't like the conclusions he'd reached. He didn't know which was worse—

continuing to believe that Ryce was just a smartass upstart, or having to come face-to-face with the level of his talents. The pilot's abilities were not only something to admire, but also something to be concerned about. People like Ryce were not readily available hands for hire for random opportunists. And if it wasn't random…

"Are you going to report the Alraki incident to the station authorities?" Ryce asked bluntly as he sat down in the second chair.

"I don't think that would be wise," Matt said.

"I thought you'd say as much, but we must report it. The Federal forces need to know that the Alraki have become so bold as to hijack ships at the heart of one of the major systems. It's dangerous to let them roam around, preying on unsuspecting civilians. You know it's the right thing to do."

Matt raised an eyebrow. "I didn't realize you were such a bleeding heart."

Ryce's expression changed slightly. "Don't you care if somebody else gets hurt because you were too afraid to say something? It would be your fault."

Being away from Ryce for a while had made him forget how irritating the man could be when he got on his self-righteous kick.

"No, it wouldn't be my fault. It would be the Alraki's fault. And it would be the Federation's fault for not watching out for them. Nobody was there to help us, remember? The only reason we're alive is because you…" He stopped and took a deep breath. "Look, I can't report it. Be realistic. What would I say? 'Hey, this Alraki ship came out of nowhere and nearly took us down, but luckily I happened to have a couple tons of explosives on board, for which I had no permit and no registration, to throw in their faces.'"

"You don't have to tell them about the explosives."

"And how am I going to explain us getting away so easily? We're not exactly a match for a frigate. It would raise too many questions. And you don't want them to look at us too closely either, if I must remind you." He lowered his voice. "Did you stop to think what the Alraki were doing in this sector anyway? There are four Fleet stations here, for heaven's sake; there are other places for them to pillage. Don't you think it's too much of a coincidence that we were attacked here, now? Your employer seemed to be convinced there were others that would try to intercept us."

"I think you're looking for excuses," Ryce said coolly. "The Alraki need no special reason to attack a solitary human ship. Trust me, if anybody is working against my employer, it wouldn't be them. They're out for blood, like they always are."

Matt shook his head. "I'm sorry. I won't risk our own safety by ratting to the authorities to ease your conscience."

"Fine." Ryce stood up. "I should have known you'd see it this way." He strode out purposefully, without looking back.

"Sorry to disappoint you, kid," Matt said to his back.

He couldn't get to the bar soon enough.

The station offered watering holes of varying degrees of repute, and Sonora Sky was somewhere in the middle of the scale. But it was where Matt felt most comfortable, and it was a good place to find jobs, useful rumors, and occasional hookups. He tended to have favorite places on all the stations they frequented, and his preferences had little to do with the decor. Sonora Sky was clean and a bit more pricey than what he was used to, but it was well liked by lower-ranking station personnel. Matt had had more than his fair share of useful connections here over a couple of beers.

He ordered a drink and took a seat at a strategic spot, listening for scraps of information in the general bustle. In the space of one hour he learned that the price of fuel had gone up in the sector, that the station commander was about to get promoted and return to the capitol, and that pirate raids were getting more and more frequent.

He was about to order another round when a woman in station uniform with a PFC insignia on the collar sat down at his table. She had a sensual curve to her mouth, and her bright red hair was pulled up in a neat bun.

"Hi, I'm Stella," she said. "Let me buy you a drink."

"Hi, Stella. I'm Matt." He cranked up his smile to its full dazzle. "I could never say no to a beautiful woman."

She ordered a round of beers and they chatted amiably for a while. Stella was funny and laid-back, and Matt liked his hookups like that. Stuck-up and judgmental was not his thing.

"Are you staying long?" she asked after Matt told her a bit about his business.

"Not really," he said. "Just passing through. So I'd hate to miss the chance to get to know you better while I'm here."

That got a flirtatious smile out of her, and they clinked their glasses.

Matt caught some movement in the crowd and spotted a familiar face there. Ryce approached the bar, a few feet away, accompanied by some guy wearing a station Federal Fleet combat pilot uniform.

For a moment, he missed what Stella was saying. What the hell was Ryce doing here? He couldn't handle a child's worth of alcohol, and he'd made it perfectly clear he wasn't interested in casual dating. And if this wasn't casual dating, it was even more suspicious, given that Matt was pretty sure Ryce at the very least had had military training, and at the worst—still was military. He had no idea why a military pilot would be involved in something so questionable as their current job, but he'd had enough experience with both the Federal Fleet and black market interstellar traffic to realize there was more to this job than he'd originally been told.

"Another round?" Stella suggested.

He snapped his attention back to her and smiled.

"The drinks are shit, but the company's too good to say no," he said and waved to the waitress. Ryce and his friend settled on their bar stools, talking softly. Matt strained to overhear them, but they were sitting too far away, and the background music and general noise made it impossible to catch snatches of conversation. What if Ryce chose to ignore his warnings and tell the authorities about the Alraki ship anyway?

"Cheers to that," Stella said as the waitress placed the drinks in front of them, and they touched glasses again.

The other pilot threw his head back and laughed at something Ryce said. They sure looked chummy. Did they know each other? Ryce didn't strike him as someone who would have a lot of friends, but perhaps he was being unfair. Perhaps there were people who found Ryce's blend of arrogance and aloofness appealing.

"Is everything okay?" Stella asked.

Matt tore his gaze away from the pilots.

"What? Oh, yeah, sure. I guess I'm just tired. Long haul and all." The hell was wrong with him? Here he was with a lovely, engaging woman, with a definite possibility of their impromptu date progressing further, and what was he doing instead of charming her pants off? Worrying over why the guy he disliked was speaking to someone else on his own free time. Okay, maybe not really disliked, but a guy whom he had no business thinking about.

"That's too bad," she said, looking slightly disappointed. "Anyway, my shift starts soon. Why don't you give me a call later?"

"Sure," Matt said, offering what even he knew was a lame smile. He entered her number into his commlink, and she got up. There was a missed call from Tony, but he ignored it. His preoccupation with their client's point man was nothing short of embarrassing. Tony wouldn't let him live this one down if she caught wind of it.

"See you later, handsome," Stella said as she walked away.

But Matt was already swiping the table touch panel to pay for the drinks, and getting up hurriedly with his unfinished beer. He wasn't exactly sure what he was going to do, but he had to at least try to get some idea what the two pilots were talking about. If it was a date, well, that certainly would be a blow to his ego, but if it wasn't... He'd had enough of the Federal military to last him a lifetime; he didn't want it meddling in his job. If Ryce was plotting something, he could find himself another ship and another runner to take his crap.

The place was crowded enough for him to approach the bar without the pilots noticing him right away. He leaned sideways on the bar, facing away from them and pretending to sip his beer, but listening intently.

As far as he could tell, the other pilot was doing most of the talking, and it centered mostly on his expected promotion.

"It's been two years on the 16," he was saying. "It's all right, but there aren't a lot of possibilities, not a lot of excitement. I don't want to be on station patrol duty for the rest of my life."

Ryce's reply was lost as someone shoved Matt's arm unceremoniously, making him lose his balance and the thread of the conversation. He grabbed at the bar top and turned around furiously, ready to take his frustration out on the clumsy idiot, but the words died in his mouth.

"Well, if it isn't the dashing Captain Spears," the man in front of him said with the slightly drawling accent common to Sonora. He was altogether unremarkable—medium height, medium build, unmemorable face. Still, Matt knew him very well, and definitely hadn't expected meeting him here right now. Pat Gentry, on the other hand, looked entirely too pleased.

"Hey, Pat," Matt said, aiming for nonchalance and doing his best to ignore the two rather large gentlemen flanking Gentry on either side. "Long time no see."

"My thoughts precisely," Gentry agreed. "In fact, I've been looking for you for a while now. When I saw the name of your ship on the registry, I had to pay a visit, considering you seemed to forget to contact me yourself. Your lovely assistant claimed she had no idea where you were, but the station isn't really that big."

Matt's guts twisted unpleasantly. Damn, Tony had probably been trying to warn him. What if they tried to hurt her? Not that he wasn't reasonably sure Tony could take care of herself, but nobody threatened his crew and got away with it. Not even Pat.

"Well, you found me," he said lightly. He sneaked a glance at Ryce, who for now continued to seem oblivious to Matt's presence and predicament. But they were standing way too close, and the menacing scowls of Gentry's bodyguards were bound to eventually draw attention. Matt really didn't want Ryce, or worse, Freeport military personnel, getting in the middle of this. They'd better wrap it up quickly.

"Where's my shipment, Spears? The deal was you unload it as soon as you get here. These things require special logistics, you know. We wouldn't want any accidents happening to the customs officers."

"Yeah, about that... There was a problem with the shipment."

Pat didn't look surprised. "I'm listening."

Mat donned an apologetic smile.

"The thing is, we ran into some trouble on our way here from Sonora-2. An Alraki frigate tried to take us down." He lowered his voice. "We had to use the cargo as makeshift IED to fend them off. It's all gone."

"You used my cargo to fight the Alraki? I'm supposed to believe this crap?" Gentry was definitely annoyed now. Matt couldn't really blame him; it was a wild tale if he ever heard one. He probably wouldn't have believed it himself.

"It's the God's honest truth. I wouldn't make something like that up. It was the only way we could get away; you know how tenacious those sons of bitches are. We barely made it out as it was."

"Even if the entire Alraki fleet was chasing you, I don't give a fuck. I paid you to run a shipment, and you failed to deliver."

"It's more of a temporary setback..." Matt began, but Gentry wasn't interested in hearing him out.

"Temporary nothing. That was twenty-five thousand creds' worth of goods you were hauling, and I needed them here on time." He let that sink in and then continued, "Now, I'm a businessman. And while nobody would blame me for being upset with you in this situation and seeking retribution, I prefer to be reasonable. All I want is be reimbursed for my cargo and for my valuable time. Oh, and let's not forget compensation for the resulting mental anguish."

Damn it. Matt really wasn't counting on that.

"I'm sure we can work something out," he said in a placating tone, while desperately trying to figure out how to get himself away from this mess. "I can make another run to fetch a new shipment for you, all costs covered. How about that? You get your goods; everybody's happy."

"I don't think you fully grasp the situation," Gentry said. He wasn't smiling anymore, and there was a cold gleam in his eyes as he leaned closer to Matt, his voice rising. "You wasted my time with this fuckup, and you owe me twenty-five grand for the cargo. With the added exemplary damages, I'll round that up to forty thousand total. And I want to be paid now."

The number was like a punch in the gut. There was no way Matt could fork over that kind of dough, certainly not at such short notice, but Gentry was not the kind of guy that would accept a payment installment plan.

Out of the corner of his eye, Matt saw Ryce finally looking in their direction and doing a sort of a double take when he recognized Matt. Ryce frowned and said something to his pilot buddy, who turned around to look at them. Fuck, Matt really didn't need any spectators right now. He shot Ryce a warning look, hoping that the kid would take the hint and mind his own business.

"Look, Pat," he said, turning his attention back to Gentry and his pals. "That's a lot of cash, and I don't have all of it right now, but I got this good-paying run. I can pay you as soon as I'm done with the job."

"Don't pull that shit with me, Spears," Gentry said. "I don't care about your runs. I want my money. You leave the 16 without paying; you don't get a second warning. Do I make myself clear?"

"Is there some problem here, gentlemen?"

The station pilot approached their little party, looking sternly between Matt and Gentry. Ryce was hovering behind him, keeping at a safe distance.

"Not at all, officer," Gentry said, pulling back from Matt, unperturbed. "We were just having a friendly chat, weren't we?"

"Sure," Matt said, pushing away his half-empty bottle. "Very friendly."

"We'll be in touch, Spears," Gentry promised, and turned away, henchmen in tow. The crowd parted almost imperceptibly before them and closed in their wake, leaving Matt to deal with the fallout.

Chapter Six

There was an awkward silence.

"This is Captain Spears of the *Lady Lisa*," Ryce said finally, when it became clear no explanation of the earlier scene was forthcoming. "And this is Lieutenant Coulson."

"Nice to meet you," Matt said curtly, making no motion to shake the man's hand. Station personnel or not, this guy had no right to interfere. It's not like they were brawling in the middle of the bar, and now Gentry was probably even more pissed off at being interrupted in the middle of his intimidation routine. And Ryce had no business sticking his nose where it fucking didn't belong and bringing his fucking serviceman buddy into the mix.

The silence stretched on.

"I have to report for duty," Lieutenant Coulson said finally, turning to Ryce. "It was nice meeting you here. We should catch up again before you leave." He nodded politely to Matt and was off.

Matt could feel Ryce's gaze on him as he pointedly examined the bottle label. It was amazing how much crap could be stuffed into the ingredients of one beer.

"What was that about?" Ryce asked, propping an elbow on the bar counter and apparently refusing to let the matter go.

"It was private," Matt said pointedly. "And whatever it was, I don't appreciate you meddling."

"I didn't meddle."

"No, you sicced your friend on me. Care to explain why you're such close pals with a Federal Fleet pilot?" He knew he was being childish, and that he was annoyed beyond what could be considered reasonable under the circumstances, but he couldn't help but feel affronted. What could that pilot hotshot boast that Matt couldn't? A rank and a uniform? If that was all it took, Ryce was in for a surprise.

"I didn't 'sic' anyone," Ryce said patiently. "It looked to me like you were in a clutch and that you might appreciate someone coming to your rescue."

"Rescue? Did it look like I needed rescuing?"

"Yes."

Matt was at a loss at how to respond to that. While Ryce's intentions might have been good, he certainly wasn't going to thank him for getting him in even deeper shit with Gentry and possibly putting him on station security's radar. Weren't they supposed to keep a low profile here, on their oh-so-secret mission? Fraternizing with military personnel didn't exactly fit into the game plan. Unless, of course, the military was actually behind the plan.

"It was nothing," Matt said finally and pushed his long-suffering bottle away. The beer was already stale by now, and he needed something stronger. "The job comes first anyway. And speaking of the job, your employer was very specific about wanting me to avoid any encounters with the Federal Fleet along the way. You should remember that before you go handing your buddy our flight report."

"All right," Ryce said. "In case you're wondering, I didn't tell him anything about…about what happened en route. And I didn't tell him who you were. I only wanted to help." He was still looking at him, for all the world like he was concerned.

"Who was that guy, anyway?" Matt asked as the pause threatened to become uncomfortable again.

"He's just a friend," Ryce said evasively.

Right. Matt had seen Ryce in real action, and based on everything he knew about him, he was willing to believe Ryce was an ace pilot, as he claimed. But Ryce happening to be friends with career-driven Lieutenant Coulson? He'd had about enough of this bullshit.

"You're a Fleet combat pilot, aren't you?" he asked quietly.

The biggest tell was that Ryce wasn't even startled by the question.

"I don't think we should discuss this here," he said. Seeing Matt's expression, he added: "Coulson has nothing to do with what we're doing here. I knew him from the Academy. I haven't seen him for a few years, and we met by chance. He asked if I wanted to have a drink, and I said yes. That's all it was."

"Sure looked like a date to me," Matt muttered, and instantly regretted it. He was being bitter and sulky, and it was neither fair nor attractive.

Ryce's expression closed off, and he withdrew, stepping away from the bar.

"It wasn't, not that it's any of your business."

"Yeah," Matt said. It really wasn't his business. His business was much too important compared to this silly teenage drama, and he needed to get back to it. "But we do need to talk, don't we?"

"I'll meet you back on the ship," Ryce said. "Unless you pick another fight in the meantime."

"Asshole," Matt muttered under his breath as the other man walked away, but his heart wasn't in it. He really had no right to be jealous, let alone act like a weird stalker. Ryce wasn't interested, whatever his reasons, and he had to respect that and get over this silly…infatuation he seemed to have developed. And as much as he wanted to blame Ryce for his spectacular screw-up with Gentry, he couldn't fault him for using whatever resources he had available to save Matt's crew during the Alraki attack. It was certainly better than anything Matt could have done in his place.

He rubbed his forehead and swiped the countertop, ordering scotch on the rocks from the top end of the list. The golden liquid went down smoothly, leaving a soothing smoky aftertaste. It wasn't the most efficient way of dealing with difficulties, but sometimes it was all one could do to keep sane. Get hammered, sleep it off, get up, and start fresh—that had always worked for him when he found himself in a jam.

And this was a very serious jam, if he stopped to examine it closely. He'd gotten involved in a job that suddenly seemed to be some sort of covert military operation. Why the military would want to employ a small-time smuggler, he had absolutely no idea. He was at a loss as to what was going on here, and that scared the shit out of him. He'd let the credit signs blind him despite his gut telling him to take a pass. And to top it off, now he owed a hell of a lot of money to one of the most dangerous people in the sector, and he had absolutely no idea how he was going to cover the debt.

He gulped down the last of the scotch and ordered another one.

"Hey, Captain," Tony said when Matt finally dragged himself up the ramp into *Lady Lisa*'s welcoming embrace.

Tony was leaning against the wall, arms crossed on her chest and a look of stern disapproval in her eyes. She wore a holstered gun strapped to her hip, though she almost never carried a weapon on board. She had clearly been waiting for a while, and she clearly thought Matt was guilty of something. Annoyingly, she was right. He should have called her right after his little chat with Gentry and made sure she was all right, but he'd been too busy lashing out at Ryce.

"While you were out there getting drunk, Pat Gentry came looking for you. He looked pissed. Hell, even his goons looked pissed."

Matt halted in the entryway, his head spinning a little. He really, really shouldn't have had that last drink. The last five drinks. Whatever.

"Yes. Pat. He found me, all right. Luckily, he decided not to bust my kneecaps right there in the bar."

"I tried to warn you," Tony said.

"Yeah, sorry about that. Was a little distracted." He remembered Stella's enticing smile. Who was he kidding? He wasn't going to call her later.

Tony gave him a withering look, which indicated she understood perfectly well what was so distracting, and it wasn't the right sort of excuse.

"He didn't try to hurt you, did he?" Matt asked, in an attempt to divert her wrath.

"No. I guess he figured it wasn't worth his time. I'm not the one handling the accounts, after all. Though I wouldn't count on his benevolence toward any one of us if he doesn't get what he wants."

"Shit." Matt rubbed his face. This was really bad. It wasn't the first time they had done business with Pat, but up until now they had never gotten on his bad side.

"Did you tell him what happened to the cargo?"

"Yeah."

"Well? What did he say?"

"You were right; Pat wasn't impressed. He figured I'd have to compensate him. Forty thousand Fed-creds."

There was a moment of silence as Tony digested the number. It was true that she didn't handle the finances, but she had a pretty good idea of their current situation. Even with Mr. Ari's advance on this job, there was no way they could scrounge that kind of money in a short amount of time.

"Matt, please tell me you got the money. Somewhere."

"Well..."

"Matt!"

He winced at the shrill note in her voice. "Don't do that. I'll talk to Pat again, and we'll figure something out."

"Yes, because he's known as such a reasonable human being!" Tony threw her hands up in frustration. "God, Matt, we're totally screwed. Pat isn't the right guy to mess around with."

"Damn right. I like my guys taller and less prone to racketeering."

"This is not funny!"

Matt put up his hands, which resulted in him nearly falling on his face. "I know, I know. Sorry. I'll deal with it. I just need a few hours to sober up."

She pursed her lips, looking at him uncertainly.

"You could always ask Nora for the money."

"No."

"You're being irrational," she insisted. "Look, I'm not telling you to ask her to solve the problem for you, or go after Gentry. You don't even have to tell her what the money is for. I'm sure she won't mind lending you some cash..."

He cut her off. "Listen, Tony. You know I love you, but you gotta get it through your head—I'm not asking my family for help, not now, not ever. With those people, everything comes with strings attached, and I'm done groveling for their approval. This is my problem, and my fucking ship, and I'm the one who's going to figure things out. And that's the last time I want to hear you mention Nora. Got it?"

Tony stared at him as if he'd suddenly sprouted horns and fangs. She huffed in exasperation and stomped off down the corridor. Matt waited until she was safely out of earshot and then groaned and softly banged his head against the wall. He was having a very, very bad day.

☆☆☆

There were two things that never failed to instill peace in the heart of Captain Spears—coffee and starlight. Poetics aside, he simply liked sipping a strong brew while sitting alone on the bridge, looking at the stars, or, as the case was now, watching ships and barges maneuver around the station like so many tiny insects hovering around a hive. It was the perfect place to calm down and think. After a few hours of uninterrupted slumber, a hot shower, and a couple of painkillers, he felt infinitely better and more focused. He still had no idea what he was going to do, but at least now he felt he could reflect on his circumstances in a calmer manner.

However, his moments of silent meditation were brief. Ryce must have been waiting for him to wake up, because he showed up on the bridge before Matt had the chance to finish his coffee.

"Captain," he said coolly as he sat down in the copilot chair.

Matt swiveled around to face him.

"And how should I address you?" he asked. "Let me guess. Flight Lieutenant?"

Ryce sighed and pinched the bridge of his nose. Somehow he managed to make even this gesture of frustration graceful.

"Apparently I'm not very good at this," he said.

"Your problem is you're a shitty liar, and for someone on a secret mission, you're not very discreet. When you don't want to be noticed, you don't stop to reminisce about the old times with your military school buddy. A few minutes of uninterrupted eavesdropping, and I would have picked up everything you're so keen on hiding, including your real name. Ideally, you shouldn't have left the ship, not on a station full of military personnel and drifters out to make a quick cred."

"I know. But I didn't see the harm in it. I wasn't doing anything that would jeopardize the mission," Ryce protested, though he didn't look convinced on the latter part.

"Then what are you doing, exactly?" Matt asked. "I took the job, all right, but I didn't sign up for anything to do with the military. I served five years in the Fleet as a space traffic controller on a cruiser, and I've had enough of that shit. It's my crew and ship we're talking about here, and I won't endanger them because of your little games."

Ryce looked up at him in surprise. "You were Fleet?"

His incredulous expression was amusing. Matt didn't go on much about his service days, but it never failed to amaze people when he mentioned this little piece of his biography. He didn't know if he should have felt insulted or flattered.

"I keep it out of the ship records, but yeah, I was for a while. I didn't fit the required mold. I thought I could find my place there, but it didn't work out." Disenchanted with the martial ethos, as he'd called it at the height of his discontent. "Anyway, I'm not the issue here."

Ryce was silent for a few moments, gathering his thoughts, and then said:

"My employer insists on confidentiality, so I won't be able to go into much detail. That being said, you're right. I am a Flight Lieutenant in the Federal Fleet and a combat pilot, but I am not here in that capacity. I have taken an extended leave of absence, and none of my direct superiors know anything about this job."

Matt whistled. "That must be some chunk of change the guy is paying you to risk your career like that. That Mnirian crap he wants must be worth a fortune."

"I'm not doing this for money," Ryce said crisply.

"Then I'm sorry to say you're being taken for a spin. But if it's not the money, what is it then?"

Ryce seemed to think it over, but finally shook his head.

"I can't tell you that; it would be a breach of confidence. But I wouldn't get involved in something like this if I didn't believe it was absolutely necessary, even if it meant putting my career on the line. It is vital that we obtain this artifact, and that it's kept secret for the time being."

"Yes, I can believe that," Matt said. "You're one of those idealistic idiots who do what's right and all that bullshit. I wish I could tell you life doesn't work like that, but you won't hear it till said life hits you in the face." He sighed. "Fine. If you tell me the military isn't involved, then I believe you. But I have a feeling there's something else about this you're not telling me, and I'm probably not going to like it."

"Nothing else is relevant at this point," Ryce said with an air of finality. "You had some concerns about me, and you had the right to demand an explanation, which I have provided. Now we should both focus on the task at hand, which is getting to Colanta."

Matt threw his hands up. "Fine. As long as there won't be any D-class cruisers chasing us."

They both fell silent. Across the view screen before them, the station traffic moved like shiny dots, tiny against the black. Matt's coffee had gone cold, but he sipped it anyway. With the control panel turned off, the bridge was eerily dim and quiet. The peripheral lights reflected in Ryce's eyes and the metal adapters on his temples, giving them a silvery glow.

"We're doing something good," Ryce said finally, breaking the silence. His gaze caught and held Matt's. "I know it doesn't look like it at the moment, and I can't get into much detail to convince you, but I know Ari, and I know what he's trying to accomplish. All I can say is it's worth the risk for me."

Matt wished he had Ryce's faith in the nobleness of Ari's motives, but his experience had taught him it was rarely the case. Life's heavy rollers had only two major incentives—power and money. Idealism was the other players' consolation prize. Those forces were as constant as those that made the galaxies spin, and there was nothing he could do to change that. Do the job, collect the pay, and move on, he reminded himself for the thousandth time, but somehow it no longer reassured him.

"What are you going to do about that guy in the bar?" Ryce asked. "He looked...unpleasant to deal with."

Matt sighed and spun in his chair. Pining for starlight was all very well, until it was time to take on reality.

"I'll get through to him," he said. "I'm a very charming person."

Chapter Seven

Matt's charm was failing him miserably.

Of course, Pat Gentry was the sort of person who was immune to charms. His sort respected cold hard cash and brute strength, neither of which Matt possessed at the moment. Even on the tiny screen of the commlink it was obvious how displeased he was.

"Are you fucking with me, Spears?" With Gentry, there really was no need for shouting and tantrums. He didn't have to raise his voice to be threatening. Matt silently thanked his stars for not having to conduct this conversation in person, opting for the safety of his own bridge instead. It was also nice to have Val there for moral support, even if he was currently only inspecting the engine computer-wiring hub.

"Look," Matt said soothingly, "I'm not bailing on you. You'll get your money, but I can't pay with something I don't have. Yet. It'll take a week, tops, and then I'll get the cash from my client. Besides, we could work out a down payment if you want. Say, about fifteen percent?"

Val, who was shoulder-deep in the wiring panel, made a noise that sounded suspiciously like a snort. Matt glared at him.

"Do I look like a fucking bank? I don't do 'down payments,' and I don't care about your jobs and your clients. Do I have to remind you what happens to people who cross me?" Pat said. "And if you think you can run, you got another thing coming. There ain't no jumpgate far enough for you to hide at."

"Come on, Pat. You know I'm good for it. You've known me for years. Besides, where am I going to go? *Lady Lisa* is registered to the Sonora sector, it's not like—"

"Cut the crap," Gentry said dryly. "You think you're so clever, Spears, then figure out how you're going to scrape together the money. I want to see the creds in my account tomorrow. Otherwise, I swear to God, you and your crew are going to regret ever hauling your sorry asses into my station."

"Well, that's just plain stupid," Matt said, becoming increasingly annoyed. Really, it was bad business sense on Gentry's part, and if he wanted to play the bully for the fun of it, Matt wasn't about to give him the satisfaction of being intimidated. "If you want to see the money, all you have to do is wait a few days. Breaking my kneecaps might be fun, but I doubt it's worth forty thousand creds."

"I'd pay to see that," Val murmured. Matt resisted the urge to kick him. His engineer slipping and damaging the electronics was the last thing he needed right now. Though for a man his size, Val did amazingly delicate work on internal circuits.

Pat leaned forward so his face filled the screen.

"You know what, Spears?" he said, "I almost wish you would run. See how much of a smart-mouth you are when it's your time to squeal."

Matt hit the disconnect key, cutting off communication.

"Fuck you, asshole," he muttered. It wasn't incredibly smart of him, but it's not like he had any choice. He couldn't buy his way out of this mess with money he didn't have, and he didn't want to be anywhere near Gentry and his thugs when they realized Matt wasn't kidding about being broke. Right now, his best bet was to split and come back after getting the rest of his fee from his client. Hopefully, the sight of Fed-credits spilling into his account would put Gentry in a forgiving kind of mood.

"That went well," Val said, pulling out a bundle of wires. He examined them and disconnected a few from the local hub, seemingly at random.

"Could be worse," Matt said. "But to be on the safe side, I suggest we get the fuck out of here as soon as we're cleared to jump. Are all systems operational?"

"They will be in fifteen minutes," Val said. He took out a roll of wire from one of his pockets and cut off pieces to attach to the hub, replacing the ones he'd disconnected.

"I don't want to be stuck on the other side of the galaxy with no way of getting back because you decided to tinker with the generator at the last moment," Matt said testily. Val had the tendency to initiate unexpected "upgrades" at odd times, but to be fair, up until now it had never interfered with their jobs.

"Might be better than coming back here. Pat's a psychopath if I ever saw one, and I've seen my share of those," Val said, placing the hub back inside the lower panel. "I'd watch out for that one, Captain."

"Tell me something I don't know." Matt sighed. "Just make sure she's ready to go. Let's hope our luck holds a little bit longer."

The corners of the jumpgate glowed white with concentrated energy, while the space between them was a gaping hole of utter blackness against the starry backdrop. It was in fact an artificial wormhole, created by the enormous magnetic forces generated by the jumpgate, a tunnel that connected two predefined points in space. Theoretically, it was possible to connect two points in time as well, but even though all scientists agreed the jumpgates indeed had this capability, it had never been successfully realized, despite numerous experiments. Mnirian technology was widely used, but it still hadn't divulged all its secrets.

Ryce guided *Lady Lisa* into position in front of the jumpgate as directed by station control. From this distance, it was possible to distinguish the strange angular markings on the massive structure, now shadow brushstrokes against the light. Matt was once again reduced to the position of a spectator, with nothing to do but watch the fast-approaching event horizon.

It was always a frightening leap of faith, plunging into that nothingness that threatened to swallow the ship and its occupants. The knowledge that you would emerge unscathed on the other side did little to abate the primeval fear the sight evoked. Matt preferred to limit his business to the Sonora system anyway, rather than traipsing around the known galaxy. Every system had its own distinct vibe, its quirks and unspoken rules, and he liked to operate under familiar conditions. Sonora had been his stomping ground for years, aside from a few quick commissioned runs to other systems.

"Phaeton 050420 slash 11, you are clear for jump," station control announced. "Godspeed."

Matt's stomach tightened unpleasantly. He suspected it would always be like this, no matter how many jumps he'd take in his lifetime, but Ryce seemed unaffected. Perhaps his intellect held a tighter reign over his viscera than a regular person's, or perhaps his combat training left no room for instinctive balking.

"Roger, control," Ryce said and cut off outside communication. The ship picked up speed and plummeted into the blackness, sucked inside with tremendous forces that threatened to tear it apart. There was a brief moment of dizziness and disorientation, as if they were falling in all directions at once, and then they were on the other side of the infinite tunnel.

The ship slowed as the light emanating from the jumpgate structure gradually dimmed and it was once again quiescent. It was strange seeing a lone gate, with no Freeport station in its vicinity, with no traffic buzzing around it.

The change of surroundings was abrupt. The sky glowed with the subtle colors of the nebula that encompassed the neighboring star systems, and the massive bulk of the Colanta-3 planet, half-lit by its red sun, took up most of the screen. It was encircled by a narrow, but rather dense field of asteroids. The view was desolate, seemingly lifeless, though of course it was merely the perception of prior knowledge.

Matt let out a long sigh and tapped the control panel impatiently. At this point being unable to connect with the ship's computer through his adapters caused him so much anxiety that it was almost a physical pain. Ryce was perfectly capable of monitoring the ship's status, but it was more and more difficult to relinquish control, especially in such a strange setting.

Ryce zoomed in on a portion of the asteroid belt. Rocks of various sizes floated serenely around the barren planet, but upon closer inspection, some appeared to be more uniform in shape and scale, spread evenly among the more irregular ones. They were darker, and their texture looked more metallic than the surrounding rubble.

"What are those spheres?" Matt asked, already dreading the answer. He had a very bad feeling.

"Perimeter mines," Ryce said. He avoided looking at Matt, concentrating on the screen instead, where different segments of the belt were being displayed in sequence.

"Mines?!"

Ryce winced. "Obviously, this site was of importance to the Mnirians. The moon's orbit lies deep within the asteroid belt, and the mines are an additional line of defense. Like the jumpgates, they have a remote deactivation mechanism."

"And you know how to deactivate them?"

"Well, no."

Matt threw his hands up in exasperation. He knew he shouldn't have taken this job in the first place, but he'd chosen to ignore his gut instinct, and now, that decision came back to give him the virtual middle finger. What use was all that money if they weren't alive to use it? Might as well go back to Gentry and give groveling a fair chance. At least that bastard would keep *Lady Lisa* intact when he took her away from him, unlike a Mnirian perimeter mine.

"If you think we're going in there, you're crazy. We'd never make it. I did not sign up to be blown to pieces by some alien booby-trap charges."

"There's no other way," Ryce said. "The ship would be impossible to maneuver there, it's true, but a shuttle is nimble and easier to steer. It can be done."

Matt seriously doubted it. Up close and personal, the setting looked much more intimidating than on a simulated star map, which didn't even include the main feature. "Yes, I remember what you said about the shuttle, but it's still out of the question. What if these things are motion-activated? Even if they're stationary, one little mistake and we'd be splattered all over those rocks."

"You don't have to go," Ryce said, shrugging. "As I recall, your job was simply providing me with a vessel at destination point. I am perfectly capable of going in alone. If you end up losing your shuttle, I'm sure Mr. Ari would compensate you for it."

It was a perfectly reasonable suggestion, and one he should have wholeheartedly agreed to. But somehow the thought of sending Ryce alone to pick his way through the minefield, while he remained in the safety of the ship, was less than appealing.

"Whatever," he muttered, getting up. "I'll go check with Val that the shuttle auxiliary systems are operational."

☆☆☆

The fact that Ryce proposed he'd go alone so offhandedly was slightly insulting. It was as if he thought Matt lacked either the courage or the capability to take the risk. Which was irrational, since he really didn't want to go, and he seriously doubted he was going to be of any help anyway. He wasn't a combat pilot, after all; crazy maneuvering and adrenaline rushes weren't his forte. But still, it would have been nice to be considered as more than a cover name on a jump log.

Matt made his way to the rec room but found it empty. Val was probably in his cabin, but he didn't go there right away. Instead he went over to the secret compartment in the wall that housed his "liquor cabinet" and opened the sliding panel. The precious glass bottles gleamed dully in the dim fluorescent lighting. He could almost taste the familiar smokiness of the whiskey.

Ridiculous. Here he was, pouting like a child who was told he couldn't join a trip to an amusement park. What did he care, anyway? Ryce was right; his job was getting them here and back, not playing a Russian roulette version of a treasure hunt. If Ryce wanted to risk being blown to pieces, he could very well do so without Matt's help, especially after basically deceiving him about the real challenge the mission presented. It would serve him right, really, him and his asshole employer who was so nonchalant about sending a brilliant young man to his death. Matt had seen enough of this shit during his service—the top brass carelessly and needlessly sacrificing thousands of lives on their little chessboards without a second thought.

He shoved the panel closed with a little more force than was necessary.

"What's got you so riled up?" Tony asked from behind him, and he nearly jumped. He was so caught up in his pensiveness that he hadn't heard her coming down the corridor. Yeah, combat pilot he was not.

"God, what are you trying to do, give me a heart attack?" he muttered, turning around.

Tony eyed the panel of the cabinet, but thankfully offered no comment.

"What's the plan, Captain?" she asked. "This place gives me the creeps."

"Glad to hear I'm not the only one," Matt said. He gave Tony a brief and dry account of the challenge they were facing and added: "Anyway, we won't be staying here for long. We're going in, picking up whatever it is the client wants us to pick up, and getting the hell out of here."

"We?" Tony arched an eyebrow.

"Yeah. I mean, Faine and I are going in. We're taking the shuttle."

Where did that even come from? Up until this minute, he was absolutely sure he was staying put, so why would he change his mind so abruptly? Ryce sure as hell didn't need Matt to hold his hand. Risking his life out of commiseration was nuts. He had his ship and his crew to think about; they should be his first priority, not this arrogant prick.

"You're not serious." Tony said. "Why would you go? The only reason he's here, commandeering our ship, is that he's supposed to fly through that mousetrap, so why not let him do it?"

"I can't let him go alone," Matt said, surprising himself again with the honest truth. "He saved our lives before, so it seems like I owe him at least that much."

Tony looked at him with utter disbelief, and then her expression changed.

"What?" Matt said, trying not to sound guilty.

"Oh, no. Don't tell me you've fallen for him."

"Don't be ridiculous," Matt said irritably. "I haven't even touched him."

"Maybe that's the problem," Tony said. "Maybe if you'd slept with him, you wouldn't be mooning over him to the point of you pulling this kind of stupid shit. Come on, what are you thinking? Look out the goddamned window. Even if he does get you to that moon safely, who's to tell what's down there? He hasn't been there; nobody has. You said so yourself. If these crazy aliens went to so much trouble setting up a fence, who's to say they haven't booby-trapped the hell out of the place? What are you gonna do, hold his hand while you both blow up into pieces?"

She was close to shouting. While he did have a tendency to get on Tony's nerves from time to time, she was rarely this upset with him, which meant she was really worried. It was scary and heartwarming at the same time.

"I'm not mooning over anybody." Matt sat down on the battered sofa, and after a moment's hesitation, she joined him. "I might be making a mistake here, but you've seen what he's capable of. He knows what he's doing. It really isn't as dangerous as it sounds," he said with a conviction he wasn't feeling. "And besides, wouldn't you be curious? A Mnirian base, deserted for who knows how many thousands of years—uncharted, untapped. He can get whatever artifact he wants, but who says I can't take a few keepsakes for myself?"

That seemed to give Tony pause. Mnirian items, even ones of dubious provenance, commanded whopping prices on the black market. That kind of money, together with their fee for this run, would make for a considerable fortune.

"You can't just go about selling Mnirian shit in Sonora," she said, but he could see she was wavering.

"Not myself, but I know some people. Besides, it'll give us more than enough cash to get Gentry off our backs for good. Think about it."

"It isn't worth all that money if you get hurt." Tony tugged on her braid, frowning.

"Thanks, Tony," he said quietly, reaching out to touch her hand. "It means a lot. Truly. But I'm not changing my mind. I'm going."

"You're impossible, you know that? Stubborn as a mule."

"But that's why you like me, hot stuff." He winked at her, and she sighed heavily.

"God help me. Fine. Go. Ain't nothing I can say that'll change your mind anyway, once it's made up." She got up and turned to look at him. "You just better come back in one piece."

Chapter Eight

The landing shuttle was small, built and equipped for short flights in space and in atmosphere. It did have enough oxygen supply to serve as a lifeboat if necessary, as well as six designated space suits required by regulation. The crew of *Lady Lisa* had never used the shuttle for this purpose, but you never knew, and personal experience had taught Matt the value of a readily available lifeboat. Like the ship itself, it looked bulky and plain, but the engines had undergone continuous upgrades, and the thrusters were in perfect working order, as Val had assured him.

Ryce was already in the shuttle cockpit, methodically checking systems readiness. He looked up with surprise as Matt plopped into the copilot seat next to him.

"I thought you weren't coming," he said.

"Somebody's gotta make sure you don't crash my shuttle," Matt said, strapping himself into the seat. "You being used to flying a Falcon fighter and all, and not these types of floating tin cans."

Ryce smiled. It transformed his face as if a sudden ray of light had illuminated it.

"Thank you," he said quietly, touching Matt's hand.

Matt looked at his hand, and then at Ryce. It was the first time Ryce had touched him of his own volition. It felt...weird. As if he were the virgin, and the mere touch of another man sent his heart aflutter. Ridiculous. He cleared his throat and nodded at the window screen.

"If we're all set, take it out. Let's get this thing over with."

"Aye, Captain," Ryce said, still smiling. The screen grew transparent, providing them with a panoramic view. Colanta cast its reddish light into the shuttle interior, giving it an eerily alien appearance.

"Ready for takeoff," Ryce said, opening the channel to the main bridge. In their absence, or rather, in Matt's absence, Tony was left in charge. Matt suspected she wouldn't leave the bridge until they came back.

"You're all clear," Tony's voice said. "Good luck, and Godspeed."

"Roger that," Ryce said.

The shuttle lifted effortlessly from its nesting point on the sail and sped into the black, leaving *Lady Lisa* to drift alone in outer orbit. Ryce skirted the asteroid belt, aiming to avoid entering the minefield for as long as possible while approaching the moon.

"So what are we looking for down there, exactly?" Matt asked, watching the data feed on the side of the screen. The moon they were searching for was relatively small, no more than five thousand miles in circumference, and according to the shuttle scanners, they still had a long distance to cover.

"There should be some sort of a structure," Ryce said. "Our scanners should be able to pick up on it once we're close enough. We will have to go inside to look for the object."

"And what does this object look like?" Matt asked. The thought of entering what for all intents and purposes would be some sort of a secret outpost of an ancient alien race, scavenging for their leftovers, was more than a little unsettling.

Ryce glanced at him. "We will know it when we see it."

"That is very reassuring," Matt said. "In fact, I believe this whole mission is based on solid intel and a reliable plan of action. No uncertainties and hidden agendas whatsoever."

"The sarcasm doesn't help," Ryce said reproachfully.

"It's either that or quietly panicking, and frankly, I prefer the sarcasm."

The asteroids drifted in and out of their field of vision in endless succession. The moon was visible now—a massive, roughly spherical shape in the midst of a dense lattice of rocks, shrouded now in the planet's shadow. Ryce activated the long-range scanners, and they were treated to images of the moon's surface, along with a running list of specs. Not unexpectedly, there was no atmosphere and no water, just a wasteland littered with impact craters. The sight was less than welcoming, but at least there was no chance of anybody interfering.

"I have a bachelor of science degree in xenohistory," Ryce said. "I've done extensive research on Mnirian culture and technology. Trust me, I'll find what we're looking for."

"Really?" Matt said incredulously. "A degree in xenohistory?"

"Among other things, yes," Ryce said. "I also have a PhD in mathematics and degrees in physics, engineering, classical literature…"

"Yeah, okay," Matt said hastily. "I get it, hotshot. You'll know it when you see it." The sheer number of diplomas Ryce boasted made him feel kind of embarrassed about the four years it had taken him to finish his undergrad studies. Granted, he'd had a very different path set before him when he had been in college, one that hadn't included studying ancient civilizations for the fun of it.

The moon now loomed directly before them, a foreboding mass behind jumbled rows of inanimate sentinels. The shuttle slowed as Ryce reset the course.

"We're going in now, Mr. Spears," he said. He switched to manual mode and took hold of the control stick.

"I hope you spent as much time flying a Falcon as you did in the classroom, kid." God, he really didn't want to go in there. But here they were, and it was too late to admit he was scared and go back, even if he wanted to. Nothing to it, he told himself. A shuttle this small would have no difficulty flying through this maze. Unless, of course, those mines were capable of locking on to target like cruise torpedoes. Who the hell could tell what those Mnirians were thinking.

Ryce was relying on the low burn of the thrusters to guide the vessel along the rubble at a careful speed, his full attention on the screen, taking in both the visuals and the data feed. Chondritic debris and artificial metallic spheres glided along as they passed, illuminated briefly by the harsh lights of the shuttle's front projectors. The tension of the first few minutes of their progress gradually eased as it became clear the mines were most likely completely static. Had they been deactivated entirely by their makers long ago, no longer posing any real threat? Matt didn't want to test this hypothesis. A chance collision with any one of the rocks, even without detonation, would result in severe damage.

As if to illustrate his thoughts, a small boulder bumped on the underside of the shuttle, making it rattle. The control panel lights blinked in alarm, and Matt clutched at the armrests of his seat instinctively. Here was the real danger of traversing the asteroid zone. The larger rocks were easier to avoid given their dispersion and the shuttle's current velocity. The little chunks, which hardly even registered on the scanners, were more abundant and required more attention. Their impact couldn't breach the hull, but it could send them on a collision course toward a bigger one, or worse, toward one of the mines, which were only barely large enough to be picked up by the scanners.

"Easy, now," Ryce murmured as he gently stabilized the shuttle and corrected the course. He guided the spacecraft with fluid, precise movements, but their progress, due to the inability to maintain a steady course, was excruciatingly slow. It was like flying through a thick chunky soup, and not the warm, comforting kind.

The nameless moon of Colanta-3 loomed before them. Technically, it wasn't even a real moon—just a large asteroid caught in the planet's gravitational field. Its lifeless surface was riddled with scars left by other asteroids and meteorites over the millennia. There was nothing there that visibly indicated past presence of sentient life-forms. It was the most unremarkable hunk of rock. Perhaps that was the point—if Mnirians had indeed been hiding something valuable or dangerous, this wouldn't be the first place anybody would have thought to look. Just how had his client, Mr. Ari, come upon his information? Information that nobody else possessed, including the military and the academic communities. The discovery of such a landmark, if made public, would make headlines across the galaxy, and the Federation would be on it in a matter of hours. And if the military had caught a whiff of this, the place would have been kept secret and heavily guarded. So what was Ari really playing at? By sending them here, he was risking more than Matt's freedom and Ryce's career; he was edging into treason territory.

Ryce glanced at the scanner feed, which transmitted continuous data from the surface. The shuttle veered around the moon, heading for the dark side, picking its way through the mine grid.

"Ground temperature negative two-hundred and fifty degrees Fahrenheit," Matt said. "Nice and cool. I wonder if the Mnirians had to wear protective gear here too."

"I would think so. The current theory postulates they were a humanoid race, like the rest of the higher-evolved intelligent species in the galaxy."

Matt shrugged. "Who knows with them? Nobody really knows what they looked like; it's all talk and guesses. Imagine finding a Mnirian space suit somewhere down there. Or even actual remains. Can you imagine it? A Mnirian skeleton. Maybe it'll look so weird we won't even realize what it is if we see it."

He had to stop himself; rambling wasn't going to make things better. And he wasn't sure what was worse—coming all this way to find nothing at all, or finding something he didn't really want to see.

"The scanner isn't detecting anything irregular above ground," Ryce said, frowning slightly. "We'll have to go around the moon and see if we can pick up on something. The scanners on this thing aren't very powerful."

"It's a basic shuttle, not an exploration vessel," Matt said, a tad defensively. "And that thing is big. It'll take time to process the readings."

"Yes, you're right," Ryce said, and the feed disappeared from the screen.

"Hey!" Matt leaned forward in his chair. "What did you do?"

"I don't want to wait for the processing. I can receive the raw data through the adapters."

Matt looked at him in astonishment.

"Receive the raw data... Are you insane?! You're flying the goddamned thing! You want to sift through thousands of surface readings in your head while trying to avoid being blown up by a bomb the size of a watermelon? That's what the fucking computer is for!" This was really too much. He was willing to put up with a lot of shit, but this crossed the line. He wasn't about to die simply because Ryce had overestimated his own capabilities.

"Would you please calm down?" Ryce said levelly. His hand was still steady on the control stick, and he didn't look dazed by the inflow of information into his brain, but all it would take was one slip, one fraction of a second of not paying enough attention. "If you're trying to make a case against possible distractions, you freaking out isn't exactly helping."

"You're going to get us killed! I don't care what kind of a genius you think you are, but I'm not—"

"Wait," Ryce said in a different voice, cutting Matt off. "There it is."

"There what is?"

"The base."

"What?" Matt frowned, surveying the moon's image on-screen. "I don't see anything."

"It's underground. There seems to be a network of tunnels running just below the surface. A slight irregularity to the ground density in a structured pattern."

Matt stared at him. "The computer would have analyzed that," he said finally.

"Yes, but it would have taken time for it to recognize a pattern in a random array of numbers with no set search parameters. We were looking for a visible structure, not a subterranean complex." He glanced at Matt. "It was quicker this way."

Matt closed his eyes and rubbed his temples, around the adapters. The cash, he reminded himself, think of the cash.

"Just get us there, will you? Let's hope they didn't lay land mines as well. Otherwise it'll be one hell of a landing party."

☆☆☆

The entrance to the network of tunnels, which according to Ryce constituted the Mnirian base, was nothing more than the gaping mouth of a cave. Ryce lowered the shuttle past the last line of rubble and mines and glided over the moon's surface, looking for a place to land. Despite Matt's private fears, the scanner didn't register anything remotely resembling explosive charges on the ground. That wasn't surprising—even the most paranoid builders wouldn't want underground tunnels crushing down on their heads after an intruder-triggered explosion.

There was nothing to indicate any sort of a landing pad near the entrance, so they had to improvise, finding a relatively flat and level spot. The shuttle's projectors illuminated the craggy ground below. It wasn't until the shuttle touched ground and came to rest on its shock absorbers that Matt could finally let go of the armrests he had been clutching. Not being able to directly monitor the performance of the landing gear was almost as bad as being cut off from the flight computer.

The projectors focused on the cave, which was nothing more than a large open hole in a clustered rock formation. There were no visible traces of foreign architecture anywhere in its vicinity.

"Are you sure this is the place?" Matt asked doubtfully. Ryce had found the subterranean tunnels, but he could be wrong about their artificial origin.

"If it isn't, we're going to find out soon enough," Ryce said. He switched back to automatic control and sat back heavily, rubbing his neck. It gave Matt a strange sort of satisfaction seeing him display at least some human weakness, however small. Maneuvering a shuttle through an obstacle course must have been a lot more difficult than handling an agile Falcon in open space.

He contacted the ship to let Tony know they'd arrived safely and were going in, and went to get his space suit out of its plexiglass compartment in the entryway.

They hadn't had many opportunities to use the space suits on *Lady Lisa*, since most of their jobs didn't require open space salvage, but it was good to have them on hand, as the case was. The suit felt flexible but heavy as he pulled it on. The oxygen generator, with its batteries, added to the weight, but it was completely autonomous and allowed for at least forty-eight hours of active wear. Matt hoped they wouldn't need it for that long. He turned off the reflective visor on the helmet, figuring they wouldn't need its protection while underground. On the other hand, the helmet-mounted lights and the thin luminous strips inside the headgear should prove more useful in presumably lightless surroundings.

Ryce was as meticulous about inspecting the suit as he was about checking the shuttle, though Val had already tested the suits prior to their departure. The delay grated on Matt's nerves a little, but he couldn't fault Ryce for being thorough, especially when their lives depended on the suits' performance in a hostile environment.

They activated the high beams of their helmet lights as they made their way from the shuttle to the cave. Their graviboots augmented the moon's gravity, which was a mere fraction of the standard 1 g force, keeping them grounded with a convenient degree of pull. The entrance looked no different from the surrounding landscape, and as they came closer, the lights touched on bluish and silvery streaks of silicates that gave the dark stone a more vibrant appearance.

The harsh lights emanating from the sides of their heads made a path for them as they headed into the cave. The uneven ground slanted downward in a gentle slope. The silence, so complete after the background humming of the engines and the control notifications, was broken only by the sound of their breathing over the internal communications channel.

The decline became steeper even as the cave floor became smoother. Light beams danced as they made their way along the tunnel, casting jerky shadows on the walls.

"There," Ryce said suddenly, just as Matt was about to question their going farther. The cave ended in a set of large double doors about twelve feet tall. He stopped, and his helmet light slid on the smooth surface, which reminded him instantly of the slickness of the original Mnirian jumpgates. There was only a thin, hairlike fissure running down the length of the doors to indicate where they would open.

Ryce went up to the doors and ran a gloved hand over the dark gray stone, or what looked like stone. His fingers left trails in the thick layer of dust.

"How are we going to get in?" Matt asked.

"I assumed the mechanism on whatever portal we encountered would operate by the same principles as the jumpgates," Ryce said. He turned slowly, looking up. The silver corners of the doors gleamed, exhibiting the same angular script found on most Mnirian relics. Matt really didn't know much about their civilization other than the most common facts, and right now, he wished he'd picked up a few relevant courses in college.

Ryce carefully took a small device out of his hip pack. Matt hadn't seen him carrying it before. It was roughly the size of a commlink, with a wide screen, but was bulkier and had four small lens tubes mounted on the underside.

"What's that?" he asked, nodding at the thing.

"A laser generator," Ryce said. "Mr. Ari and I had agreed we'd need one if we ever got to this point."

"So it's like spacecraft jumpgate activation tech?"

"Something like that. Only on a much smaller scale."

Laser technology was crucial to operating the jumpgates, yet here they were, facing a regular door. Okay, maybe not that regular, considering the location, but it certainly wasn't an apparatus designed to fold space and time. However, from his brief acquaintance with Mr. Faine it was clear the man never did anything without thinking it through, no matter crazy it seemed. Not like they had an array of other options to open the door, so whatever Ryce was trying, Matt was willing to play along.

Ryce pointed the laser at the door. The lens tubes swiveled into position, and four bluish beams shot out at precise angles, touching the four corners of the portal. The silver metal began to glow, absorbing the energy, and the markings on it deepened, standing out in stark relief, waiting to be activated. Matt didn't know whether they were letters, numbers, or hieroglyphics.

"How do you know the right sequence?"

"I don't know for sure. The language is not fully decrypted yet." Ryce studied the markings and adjusted the laser beams to point at specific symbols. "But I can make a few educated guesses."

The doors remained closed, and Ryce frowned. His breathing was calm and even over the comm as he tried more and more combinations, pointing the beams at different symbols in rapid succession.

The sudden motion caught Matt by surprise. The metal corners flashed white, and the doors opened silently outward, startling both of them.

Ryce glanced at Matt and turned off the laser. The doors remained open, revealing a dim cavernous space beyond.

"Shall we?" Without waiting for a response, Ryce stepped through the doorway, and Matt followed him a heartbeat later.

Chapter Nine

The beams from their helmets cut through the dimness of a huge hall. It was long and narrow, running perfectly straight and bearing no resemblance to the natural cave outside. The dark walls had the same slightly oily sheen as the doors. The ceiling, supported by two rows of smooth unadorned columns, was a perfect reflection of the floor. A thick layer of dust covered everything, and their graviboots left footprints as they crossed the hall. So far, nothing spoke of the purpose of this place. It might have been illuminated somehow in the past, but there were no black and silvery writings on the walls, or anything that resembled machinery or a control console of any kind. Matt just hoped there were no nasty surprises waiting in the gloom for them. His imagination did him no favors though, as bits of scenes from old horror movies he'd seen looped helpfully in his mind. There were always those idiots who went into some abandoned mansion or alien ship, sparing no thought for the possible dangers lurking there, and they always regretted it just before all hell broke loose and they died in an inevitably gruesome way.

You're not in some cheap movie, he reminded himself sternly. It's a salvage mission. There were no aliens here, and he didn't believe in ghosts and boogeymen. All they had to do was keep their eyes open and be on alert. The worst that could happen would be ending up stuck in front of a door even Ryce couldn't open. And either way, he was going to get his fee.

"It's like walking into a tomb," Ryce said suddenly, and Matt turned to him in surprise. Ryce caught his gaze and shrugged. "It's so strange here. Feels...wrong to come in. Disturbing the dead, even if they're not here."

Matt was a bit perplexed by Ryce's unexpected sensitivity; he was always so mission-oriented, and not easily spooked. The structure was a little eerie, that was true, but mostly it was just...empty. "If this Ari, whoever he is, found this place, others would have found it eventually. Might as well be us, right?"

Ryce shrugged again, his light scanning the far wall as they crossed the hall. "There should be another door, or some sort of opening," he said, changing the subject. "This can't be it. There are at least four or five tunnels running underground, if my analysis is correct."

Matt refrained from questioning the accuracy of his evaluations. "Okay, let's look for it," he said, wandering off to study the walls. They all appeared exactly the same to him—void of any external markings or cracks that would indicate a possible opening. He turned to the dusty floor, his light following. "Maybe there's a kind of a trapdoor," he said. "The tunnels probably run deeper than this level."

Ryce directed his gaze onto the floor as well, adding more illumination. "It's hard to see," he said. "But you may be right. This chamber is not that deep."

They retraced their steps, this time paying closer attention to the floor, until they stood in the center of the hall. Ryce knelt and examined the surface.

"There's definitely something here," he said. "Some sort of pattern."

Revealing it proved to be a tedious task, which had them crawling on the floor wiping away the dust as best they could. There were delicate lines etched into the black stone, forming a large circle, about six feet in diameter, with symbols running around its border. The center was filled with jumbled geometric shapes that made no sense to Matt. It hurt his eyes a little when he tried to follow them too closely, so he concentrated on the more familiar symbols.

"What does it say?" he asked. It was hard to believe that a degree in xenohistory would ever prove useful in real life, but he had to admit Ryce had an advantage here. Scavenging at Mnirian sites was much easier with somebody who understood what little had been deciphered of their language.

Ryce rose to his feet, dusted the pants of his suit unnecessarily, and walked around the circle, muttering something under his breath.

"I think it's a kind of platform," he said. "Like a freight elevator that goes down a bore cut into the rock to the lower levels. See, there's a crack that runs around the edge."

"Can you activate it?"

"I can try." Ryce paced around the edge of the circle again. His boots left crisp markings in the dust. "The mechanism looks different than the doors."

"Take your time. It's not like we're in a rush." Matt adjusted his helmet light, pointing it straight at the pattern so Ryce could have a better view. Despite his assurances, he really didn't want to spend more time here than was strictly necessary. He couldn't help but think they'd gotten in too easily. This was supposed to be a secret base. Considering the perimeter mines around the moon, maybe even a military base. If the Mnirians even had a military. But regular human Fleet bases had more efficient security measures installed than this. It made him nervous, wondering if they were missing something in their eagerness to reach the prize.

Ryce didn't comment. He squatted in the middle of the circle, fiddled with his laser device, and set it up on the floor. Matt watched as three laser beams shot out across the floor, touching on three different symbols. The etched lines glowed, but everything remained motionless. Ryce frowned and tried again, and then again with no results.

"What's wrong?"

"I told you, the mechanism is different." Ryce turned the device off. "Direct excitation won't work here."

"I thought all their tech was laser-based," Matt said, walking up to him. If Ryce couldn't crack the combination and get them inside, there was nothing for them to do here. The hall was entirely empty of anything else but the columns. And as much as he didn't like returning to a client empty-handed, he had to admit he would be more than a little relieved at not having to go farther into this place. Besides, the deal was that Matt only provided the means of transportation. He'd still get paid whether they turned up with the artifact or not.

"It is, but it's more complicated than simply pointing a laser at the right symbol. I have to figure it out somehow." Ryce sounded flustered. He was probably not used to being wrong or failing at something. Too bad they were too preoccupied at the moment; Matt could have taught him all about that. He was practically an expert at it.

Stepping around the circle again, Ryce peered at the symbols more closely, and then he crouched, almost crawling on the floor on top of the entangled figures, tracing them with his gloved fingers.

"I really doubt you're supposed to do that," Matt said, watching him.

"There must be something else here," Ryce said stubbornly. "This is the way down, I'm sure of it."

"I'm not questioning it, but if we can't get in..." He had a feeling Ryce wouldn't give up so quickly, but he wished they could just go.

Ryce paid no attention to that. He almost pressed his helmet to the floor to get a closer look at something at the center of the circle.

"Look. I think I've found it."

"What is it?"

"A keyhole."

"A keyhole. Seriously? Now we need a...what, a skeleton key to open this thing? What happened to all that advanced high-techy stuff?"

"Not an actual keyhole," Ryce said impatiently. "A point to focalize energy. I've been trying to open it with synchronous beams, like a gate, but this thing requires the beams to converge into a single point and transmit below. I'll have to reconfigure this."

He set up the laser device on the floor again and fiddled with the settings. At one point, he huffed with annoyance, took out a screwdriver from his suit's emergency kit, and took the device apart, continuing his tinkering on the inside. Matt rolled his eyes, but there wasn't much he could do to either help or dissuade Ryce from trying to do his thing. Personally, he didn't like the idea of playing with powerful lasers with barely any equipment on hand, but he wasn't the boy genius.

Finally, Ryce seemed satisfied with whatever he'd done to the laser, and stood up.

"Here, help me with this."

They both held the device a few feet above the ground, positioning it exactly atop the keyhole, which to Matt's eyes was nothing more than a tiny oval-shaped indentation at the intersection of several lines within the pattern.

"It won't burn a hole through my foot, will it?" Matt asked, doing his best to hold the laser as far away from his body as possible.

"Not unless you point it there," Ryce said. "It's very precise. Ready?"

No, he wanted to say, but he simply nodded. Ryce activated the laser and tapped on the tiny screen in quick succession. Three beams shot out, touching the same symbols on the outer rim of the circle as on the first try. The symbols flickered and glowed again. Ryce touched the screen again, and the glow intensified. Another beam shot down from the device into the keyhole point.

That thing sure came in handy, Matt thought as he peered at the screen. In itself, a laser, even a converging one, wasn't a very complex thing, but this generator was apparently specifically modulated to be compatible with Mnirian technology. It wasn't something one could purchase over the counter; a lot of research had to have gone into it. Very specific applicative type of research.

He didn't have time to take the thought further, as the entire pattern suddenly came to life, the intricate lines shining brightly against the dark stone. A slight vibration started up under his feet, as if some unseen gears had been set into motion, and the portion of the floor they were standing on shook gently.

Matt wobbled unsteadily, the movement catching him off guard. The laser shifted—thankfully not enough to hit his foot; but it didn't matter anymore. The mechanism was activated and the circle, now a platform, slowly slid down, inching past the level of the floor.

"Stop being right all the time. It's annoying as hell," Matt said as Ryce turned off the device and pocketed it.

"Sorry," Ryce said, but he was smiling, and there was smugness in his voice. Matt couldn't help smiling back at him.

The platform descended about sixteen feet through the mass of rock when the bore slowly opened up to a bigger space. It finally came to rest gently, once again a scribed circle, flush with the lower floor. They were now standing in a tunnel about ten feet wide, with the bore looming into the darkness over their heads. Before them, the tunnel ran from the point of the platform in opposite directions. The walls were hewn out of the same black rock as the rest of the place, perfectly incurvated, at least twelve or thirteen feet high. The light from the helmets bounced off the smooth surfaces and was swallowed in the perpetual gloom that lurked in the distance.

"Very minimalistic," Matt observed.

"There are gas traces here," Ryce said, pulling the environmental data from his helmet scanner. "Nitrogen, methane, helium, oxygen. Not enough for an atmosphere; certainly not breathable. Could be the product of radioactive decay in the moon's core being trapped here on the way to the surface."

"I'll be sure not to take the suit off to get a whiff," Matt said. "Which way should we go now?"

They turned around on the platform, peering in one direction, and then the other. From what little they could see, the tunnel looked exactly the same in both directions.

"Wanna flip a coin?" Matt suggested. He'd never actually held a coin, but surely they could find something equally as random in their kits.

"Let's try this way," Ryce said, stepping forward after checking his scanner again. "Northeast."

Matt shrugged and followed him, glancing behind as they went on. The platform remained motionless, the etched pattern with the keyhole now marking the tunnel floor directly beneath the bore. Soon it was lost from view in the darkness and as the floor continued to slope down a few degrees. Though the concave ceiling was high, it was easy to remember they were traveling deep underground, with thousands of tons of rock above their heads. Matt was never afraid of tight spaces (after all, he was used to being cooped up in a spaceship for long periods of time), but here he could well understand the cliché about feeling the walls closing in. Maybe it wasn't so much about claustrophobia as worrying the freaking tunnel would come crushing down on them. It wasn't as if it had been subjected to maintenance any time recently.

Despite his concerns, there were no visible signs of corrosion or decay. The tunnel ran in a slight but steady decline, and nothing hindered their progress. They saw no cracks or openings along the way, no writings or symbols, only the same thick layer of dust on the floor.

The distance meter showed they had covered about fifteen hundred feet when the tunnel ended abruptly, opening into another chamber. It wasn't as large as the pillared hall above, but was round and had a vaulted ceiling, so high that the helmet beams could barely reach it.

Six pillars, spaced evenly apart, protruded from the walls. Soaring upward, they formed sharp ridges that spanned the dome above. As with everything else they'd seen so far, the walls appeared to be solid stone. The floor was different, however; it was made of some sort of dull metal, every inch of it etched with shapes and angular characters.

At the center of the room was a rotund raised plinth, about three feet in diameter. A ring of deeper etching ran around its base, the symbols there glowing faintly on their own. It was the first kind of "natural" lighting they'd seen since entering the cave. It gave the chamber a sinister feel, as if the dark shadows that had lingered there for eons suddenly slithered to life with the random passing of their light beams.

Ryce stepped farther into the room, looking around. A narrow rectangular door stood opposite the entrance. It was of a familiar configuration, similar to the main double gates in the cave, with metallic laser receptor corners. He didn't approach it right away but instead turned his attention back to the central plinth. Matt followed him, coming to stand by his side as they both looked at what was mounted on it.

At first Matt didn't understand what it was. A narrow metal cylinder protruded from the plinth, going up and disappearing into the ceiling. Its base, which rested on the plinth at the level of their chests, was enveloped in dark metallic blocks inscribed with writing. They appeared to be some kind of machinery. The blocks were irregular in shape and size, and the etchings on each of them varied in density. Some symbols seemed to repeat over and over again on different blocks, but Matt lacked the expertise to notice any subtle differences, if there were any.

Ryce ran his hand over the face of one of the blocks. The symbols glowed dully under his touch, which nearly made Matt jump.

"Why is it doing that?"

"I don't know. The mechanism could be heat sensitive to some degree. Looks like it could be a control panel." Ryce gave the blocks an experimental push, and they parted under his hand, revealing a shallow cavity, about a foot long, filled with narrow vertical ridges. Ryce tapped one of the ridges cautiously, but nothing happened.

The longer they stood in the room, the more convinced Matt became they shouldn't be there. It was wrong to be here somehow, though he couldn't quite explain it. It wasn't the superstitious fear of stealing from the dead. They weren't raiding a tomb, whatever Ryce had said, and it wasn't as if the long-gone builders could protest them being there. But the sense of wrongness persisted. It was this thing, this machine in the middle of the room that made him nervous. At this point, it was silly to be spooked by Mnirian technology, because so far all they'd done was open doorways and find their way around. But this thing, whatever it was, gave him the heebie-jeebies, and suddenly Matt didn't want to find out what it was.

Ryce, on the other hand, seemed fascinated with it. He walked around the plinth, carefully examining each block and the surface of the cylinder itself, his face animated with something close to awe.

"I've never seen anything like it," he murmured.

"What is it?" Matt asked. He glanced around uneasily, but there was nothing around them but silent shadows. He couldn't shake the feeling they were being watched.

Ryce looked up, and his light showed the end of the metal cylinder. Matt followed it with his gaze. Even with his added light, the beams came just short of touching the highest point of the domed ceiling.

"It's a cannon."

"A cannon?" The mere simplicity of the concept left him baffled. He'd never seen a Mnirian weapon of any sort; hell, he didn't know if such things even existed. And if they did, he imagined they would be as bizarre and extraordinary as the jumpgates must have seemed to the people who first discovered them. But for it to be something as mundane as a cannon?

Ryce approached the narrow door, directing the helmet light at the etched corners, and Matt followed him.

"What is it exactly we're looking for here?" he demanded. A cannon of any sort would imply this was indeed some kind of a military base, and the thought made him uncomfortable on many different levels. One of those levels being that whatever his client was after, it probably wasn't a shiny trinket.

Ryce ignored him as he took out his laser generator and directed the beams on the four metal corners. The corners glowed, and the door slid into the wall silently, opening up to another, much smaller room.

They peered into a plain square chamber with a low flat ceiling. It was empty and unadorned save for a circular design on the floor, about two feet in diameter and reminiscent of the pattern they'd seen in the entry hall above. Ryce knelt over the circle, brushing away the dust and searching for the expected keyhole.

At this point, Matt was more than reluctant to go for another elevator ride, unless it was the elevator that would take them back above ground. His trusty sense of self-preservation was yammering at the back of his head. He glanced to the sides, just to make sure nothing was creeping up from some hidden recess.

Ryce appeared to have no such issues. He adjusted the device's setting again, and motioned to Matt to come help him hold it above the tiny indentation in the center of the pattern. Matt sighed and held the generator, mindful of where he was standing. It was unlikely that Ryce would abandon his quest at this stage even if he begged him. And not having any arguments stronger than "I have a bad feeling" meant it was better to help him move along so they could wrap it up quickly and get the hell out.

They were both expecting the floor to descend, so when the platform began to go up, it caught them by surprise. Ryce, who was standing right on the edge of the pattern, lost his footing and stumbled backward, just as Matt jumped back with a curse. Dust particles swirled frantically in the jumbled light beams, while the platform slowly rose from the floor, forming a smooth black column above them.

Chapter Ten

"Shit! Are you okay?" Matt's voice sounded shaky to his own ears. Ryce nodded as he quickly regained his balance, and they both stared up at the newly erected column in the middle of the room that stopped just short of reaching the ceiling

This column was narrower than the one on which the cannon was mounted. A part of it, approximately at the level of their heads, was hollowed out, and a roughly rectangular-shaped object, about the size of a shoe, was resting inside. The top of the object was rounded, and covered in deep grooves about half an inch wide. Unlike the smooth stone all around them, its jet-black surface appeared to be rough and grained. It was like nothing Matt had ever seen before.

"What is it?" he asked. The object was displayed like a precious museum piece, and he walked slowly around the column, leaning in, trying to have a better look. There were no writings anywhere on the column or around the object, nothing to indicate its purpose or the manner of its use.

Ryce didn't answer. He shut down his laser generator and put it away before stepping closer to the column to peer at the strange object with a mix of excitement and apprehension. Ryce's face was illuminated by the harsh fluorescent light. Matt didn't doubt for one second that he knew exactly what this was.

"This is what you were looking for, isn't it?" he asked.

Ryce turned and looked at him. There was an unfamiliar gleam in his eyes, though the glare of the flashlights could have been playing tricks on Matt's perception.

"I believe it is, yes."

"What is it?" Matt repeated, more insistently. He already knew he wasn't going to like the answer. They clearly weren't here to collect pottery fragments and take pictures of native art.

"This is the real weapon," Ryce said. "The cannon in the other room is only that. A cannon. This"—he pointed at the dark object—"is the charge."

"The charge?" The only type of heavy artillery Matt was even remotely familiar with was a standard spacecraft torpedo launcher. This looked to be in a different category altogether. "You mean it's a warhead?"

"Yes, of sorts."

Suddenly, Matt had had enough. Enough of the evasiveness, the secrets, the stuck-up know-it-all attitude. Admittedly, there was something about the man that made Matt like him despite it all: Those brief moments when the mask fell away to expose the very young, lonely person underneath; those times when that same person had shown incredible courage and tenaciousness. But that fragile attraction could not hold up to the suspicion that he was partaking in something awful, something that would make the rules of their game obsolete. And no matter how partial he'd become to Ryce, or how desperately he needed the money, he could not bring himself to turn a blind eye to what was going on here.

"Ryce," he said quietly. The other man must have heard something in his voice, because he took a half-step back, eyeing him warily. "You tell me what it is and what we're really doing here, or I swear you won't be setting foot aboard *Lady Lisa* with that thing."

There was a tense pause as they stared at each other with rekindled animosity. The moment stretched on, sliding right to the edge of a precipice. Belatedly, Matt realized that Ryce had a high-powered laser within arm's reach, while the deadliest weapon in his kit was a screwdriver.

Ryce sighed and shook his head, ending the standoff as abruptly as it had begun.

"Fine, if you must know," he said, sounding more resigned than resentful. "As I said, it's a charge. A type of nuclear warhead, as you would call it, or, more accurately, an enhanced radiation weapon. Fired into the atmosphere, it would detonate in the mesosphere of a planet, the explosion triggering a reaction that would emit neutron radiation on a scale to effectively eradicate all carbon-based life-forms."

There was another pause, as Matt tried and failed to process this revelation.

"You can't be serious," he said. He looked at the black object. How could something so small be so sinister? A weapon that could wipe out all life on an entire planet with a single shot, and it was sitting there on this retractable shelf. Wouldn't a neutron warhead require more elaborate maintenance? He raked his reeling brain for crumbs of information remembered from nuclear weapons and radiation physics study. "Isn't it too old to be operational? It must have been here for who knows how long. It could be thousands of years."

"I don't know much beyond the basic description," Ryce admitted. "And most of it is pure theory. But if the theory is correct, the weapon is based on a previously unknown type of radioactive isotope with a very long half-life and high fusion-boosting potential. No other known weapon has ever come close to having such destructive power." He glanced in the direction of the cannon chamber. "Colanta-3 is all but uninhabitable, you know; most of it is a barren desert with unstable conditions. Maybe this is because it was the Mnirians' testing site."

"And you want to take it...and do what with it, exactly?" Matt asked. "This is not a souvenir you can push on the black market, is it? What does your employer want it for?"

"You were not supposed to ask questions, remember?" Ryce said brusquely. "It was a part of your contract. And since when do you have scruples, anyway? You were perfectly okay with hiding the fact the Alraki were on the prowl in the Sonora sector to cover your own ass."

"Yes, and you were the one giving me hell about it!" Matt snapped back. "I might not have scruples, but you do, or at least I thought you did. Lying about the Alraki is nothing compared to...to stealing a weapon of mass destruction!"

Stealing archaeological artifacts was one thing, but smuggling a freaking radiation bomb into the hands of an unknown party was another. Ryce being a military officer did nothing for his peace of mind. While Ryce did appear to be idealistically principled, everybody had a weakness that could be exploited, and it was entirely possible Ryce wasn't aware of how and for what purposes he was really being used by his employer. Ryce had stubbornly avoided any explanations regarding his own motives, other than the trust he placed in Mr. Ari. Matt, on the other hand, couldn't be a hundred percent sure Ari was even human, or that he wasn't going to sell this weapon on the black market, where there was no telling in whose hands it could end up.

"I'm not getting into this with you," Ryce said with finality as he turned toward the object in its cavity. "Not now."

Matt moved quickly to intercept him, shoving the other man hard. He didn't think about what he was doing, merely acted on impulse.

Stopping Ryce from taking the weapon, making sure that thing stayed on its shelf, was suddenly of utmost importance.

Caught by surprise, Ryce staggered, clutching Matt's arm, and they both collided gracelessly into the column. Ryce swore—it was the first time Matt had heard him use any kind of language—and pushed him away with unexpected force. Matt went sprawling on the floor, and Ryce spun around to reach for the Mnirian warhead on its pedestal.

Bright lights exploded all around them, lighting up the chamber and nearly blinding Matt for a second. Threadlike blue beams suddenly shot all around the charge, covering the cavity opening in a dense laser spider web just as Ryce pulled it out. One of the beams caught the sleeve of his space suit, burning a pinpoint hole in the fiberglass fabric. Matt watched in horror as Ryce cried out and went to his knees, awkwardly clutching the warhead to his chest, and at the same time, trying to cover the damage in his sleeve with the other hand. Flashing inner emergency warning lights reflected off the glass of his helmet.

"Shit!" Matt hauled himself up and rushed to Ryce's side. The laser had punched cleanly through the left arm just above the wrist and out the other side of the sleeve, at the same time staunching the wound so there was hardly any blood. However, with the suit's integrity compromised, it was a matter of minutes before depressurization and oxygen leak became critical. Matt clamped his gloved hand around the perforated sleeve, ignoring Ryce's grunt of pain, and helped him up. The laser beams around the charge cavity had gone out once Ryce removed the warhead, but now the edges of the floor around the room began to glow blue. It was impossible to tell where the light was coming from, and Matt didn't want to find out in any case.

"We have to get out of here!"

Ryce nodded, cradling the warhead in the crook of his good arm as if it were a baby, and they both scrambled toward the exit just as the entire floor was washed in blue light. They tumbled through the doorway into the cannon chamber, in time to see the column in the room behind retract and laser beams shoot up from the floor to the ceiling, crisscrossing the entire room. Matt backed into the larger chamber, turning away from the intense glare, and dragged Ryce along with him, gripping his arm so hard his own knuckles hurt. Tony's warnings about likely booby-traps sprang up in his mind. They should have known it wasn't going to be that easy to plunder a military base of any sort.

"Close the door!" Ryce panted.

"I'm a little busy making sure you don't suffocate!"

"Just close it!" Ryce set the charge carefully on the floor beside them and fumbled in his kit with one hand. He took out the laser generator and thrust it at Matt.

"I don't know how to operate it!"

Ryce grunted in aggravation and swatted Matt's hand away from his arm, clamping down around the holes with his right hand again. His face was pale and shiny with perspiration.

"You'll have to. Hold it steady, and point it at the door."

Matt got to his feet and turned on the laser. There was a coordinate wheel on the screen and an outline of the four door corners. His eyes hurt from the harsh light emanating from the smaller room, and it was getting harder to focus on the device in his hands.

"Now what?"

"Pick the coordinates 6H5, 8K4, 0X8, 3D6, and make sure it's aligned properly. Then activate it," Ryce said, his voice raspy.

Matt quickly punched in the coordinates, fervently hoping Ryce had recalled the numbers properly, and pointed the laser at the door, holding it in outstretched hands.

Four laser beams shot out of the device, touching the metal corners. The door slid shut.

The sudden darkness left him with a glowing afterimage dancing in front of his eyes. He shook his head to clear it and then switched off the generator, letting out the breath he'd been holding. Belatedly he realized he could have activated the reflective visor on his helmet to protect his eyes from the lasers. It was designed to reduce the glare of direct sunlight during a spacewalk, so it would have been opaque enough to lessen the assault on the retinas.

"Do you think that's it? It's contained?" he asked as he went down on his knees next to Ryce.

"I don't know. We better get back to the surface, though."

"Hang on, you can't be going anywhere with those tears." Matt unzipped his own kit and rummaged inside. The space suit fabric was by its nature rip-resistant, but of course it couldn't withstand a laser. Matt just needed something to stem the leak long enough to get Ryce back to the shuttle.

"Oh thank God," he muttered, fishing out a bar of acrylic putty. He smeared little pieces of the tacky stuff over the tiny holes, hoping it would be enough to hold for a while.

"Thank you," Ryce managed to get out.

"Don't mention it." Matt helped him up. "Come on, let's go."

"Wait." Ryce stooped down and picked up the warhead, gasping in pain. He stowed it carefully in his kit.

"You're not taking that with us!"

"Don't be absurd," Ryce said. "Of course I'm taking it. This is why we came here, and I'm not about to leave it after all we went through to get it."

Matt gritted his teeth in frustration, but there was no time to get into another fight over this. They were lucky the defense system in the warhead chamber hadn't killed them on the spot. Luckily, there had been a delay in the old mechanisms cranking up, but either way, they should have been more careful with something so potentially dangerous. Something Ryce wasn't doing even now, lugging that thing about like a piece of wood.

Matt put his arm around the other man's shoulders, steering him out of the cannon chamber and up the corridor. The emergency warning lights to Ryce's damaged suit had long since shut off, but a thin beeping now indicated pressure loss. At least the oxygen supply was still working properly, which should give them enough time to make their way to the upper level safely. He remembered Ryce's comments about the accumulation of poisonous gases down here. It wasn't a welcome thought.

Shadows danced frenziedly on the walls, receding before their light beams as they hurried back to the elevator platform. Nothing moved to intercept them, and no lasers suddenly erupted from the floor to hinder their escape. The commotion seemed to have been confined to that single room, now securely locked behind them.

Ryce's breathing was ragged in Matt's ears. The wound must be hurting like hell. There was a basic first aid kit in the shuttle, and hopefully once they were back on *Lady Lisa* Tony would be able to help.

"Oh, God," Ryce said quietly, suddenly stopping.

At first, Matt thought Ryce was about to keel over and tightened his grip around his shoulders. But then he saw it too. The elevator platform they'd used to descend to this level was now raised all the way back up into the bore, leaving a massive stone column right in the middle of the tunnel. There was no way out.

Chapter Eleven

They stared at the black unyielding column.

"The security system must have triggered it," Ryce said weakly. "We're trapped."

"No!" Matt advanced on the column and stalked around it, searching for some sort of control panel, or a written pattern around the base, or...something. "There must be something we can do to get it down!"

Ryce shook his head. "I think it can only be activated from the upper level. There's no way to lower it from here."

"You're the expert on Mnirian technology; find a way!" Panic was rushing in. Ryce was right; they were trapped down here, buried alive inside some godforsaken moon in the middle of nowhere. They couldn't even call for help. The suits' communications channels were only linked to each other and the shuttle cockpit, so there was no possibility of alerting the crew about their predicament. And without a shuttle, neither Tony nor Val could do much to help.

Matt kicked the smooth stone in frustration. This couldn't be it! They couldn't just die here. But they would, wouldn't they? Huddled together in the dark, dying slowly, in agony as the suits' batteries drained and the oxygen generators shut down. A stupid, pointless death. But what death wasn't pointless and stupid? The result was the same, whether it was by heroics or a freak accident.

Ryce slid down the wall and sat heavily, closing his eyes.

"Come on, you can't just give up," Matt said urgently. Ryce was the last person he'd expect to throw in the towel. He was as resourceful as he was annoying. Besides, the suits were designed to operate at full capacity for at least forty-eight hours, and they hadn't been in the base for more than five. Even with Ryce's suit compromised, there was still time to try to find their way out of here.

"I'm not giving up," Ryce said, with his eyes still closed. "I just need a minute."

Matt kicked the column one more time and then collapsed on the floor next to Ryce. They sat for a while in the complete silence, interrupted only by Ryce's heavy breathing and the beeping of his suit. Matt's own life support systems were functioning properly, and the suit's sensors were broadcasting continuous feed on the side of his helmet. The levels of gas traces around them were steadily rising, but he had no idea what it meant.

Taking a breather probably wasn't a great idea. They needed to keep moving, to have something to concentrate on other than the pain and the sickening, paralyzing fear. Was Ryce about to lose consciousness? Matt had no idea what to do, and it made him feel even more helpless. He took the other man's gloved hand in his. The putty was doing a good job at sealing the holes, but he was aiming more at moral, rather than physical, support right now. Not least because he could use some as well.

"Have you ever been to Earth?" he asked. He had to keep Ryce talking, or at least responding. To keep him focused. The thought of Earth had popped to his mind unbidden. Just another regret in the long line of his losses.

Ryce shook his head.

"I have," Matt said, leaning back. "With my family, when I was a teenager. We went on a trip to the coast. It was windy, but the sun was shining. I stood there, on the edge of a cliff, looking down at the ocean, and smelled the salt in the air. There was so much air I almost couldn't breathe it all in, but there was something so right about it—the sunlight on my face, the grass under my feet. It felt like home." He turned his head and looked at the other man. "Silly, right? It was just light. Just air. Plenty of that everywhere you go. Except here." He chuckled unhappily.

Ryce opened his eyes and regarded him silently. The pain had etched lines around his eyes and mouth, making him look haggard.

"I still dream about it from time to time," Matt said. "The green grass and the wind." The way his mother had laughed as his sister chased a butterfly. He'd never see Earth or his mother ever again. Nor anything else, for that matter, apart from black walls and ancient dust.

"I wished I could see it too," Ryce said wistfully, snapping Matt out of his reverie. "There wasn't much grass where I grew up."

Matt looked at him. How different they were. Matt's own childhood was coddled, comfortable, with not a care in the world. God, what a little brat he'd been. At exactly what point had his life taken the turn that would lead him here?

"Fuck this shit," he muttered. He was damned if he was just going to sit here, quietly waiting for the air to run out, and watch Ryce slip away. No matter how angry he was at the guy for concealing something so vitally important from him, he didn't want him to die. They couldn't lose hope so soon, not without a fight. He stood up, casting about with his helmet light as he looked around.

"You said there were more tunnels here, right? Maybe one of them has a back door. An emergency exit. All military installations have escape routes, superior species or not. We can at least go look."

Ryce grunted in agreement and rose to his feet, using the wall for support.

"There is that other tunnel we haven't checked yet. There might be more at lower levels, but I haven't seen any means to get there."

"Okay," Matt said, livening up. He waved in the direction opposite from where they had come earlier. It was the only option, wasn't it?

They started down the corridor. It ran in the same gentle decline as the other one. They inspected the walls and the floor more closely this time, in hopes of finding the outlines of a door or a hatch that would lead up or into a different tunnel, but as far as they could see, there was nothing to indicate any exits. The light from their helmets now seemed feeble, unable to completely dispel the oppressive darkness that was closing in on them. Despair made the shadows tangible, like creatures that crept behind them, haunting their footsteps, threatening to pounce if they made the wrong move.

It was a relief to reach the end of the tunnel. It opened up to a round chamber, a twin to the one they had found on the other end, including another narrow door. Again, six pillars, like the bony ridges on the back of a prehistoric reptilian monster, were embedded in the walls, supporting the high domed ceiling that encompassed another huge cannon.

Matt approached the cannon plinth and ran his hand over the control blocks. They lit up and shifted slightly, just as they'd done in the first chamber.

"Why would they need two of these?" he wondered aloud.

The beam from Ryce's headlight followed the long barrel up and then leapt across the walls, but no other control mechanism was revealed.

"Maybe it's a backup," he said with some effort. "Maybe they're different in some way, and they were testing both. Maybe they built them to be used only once. Or maybe two is a lucky number."

Matt barked a laugh. "Either way, we're not taking another warhead with us, even if there is one. Not being incinerated on the spot the first time was a fluke; I'm not risking that again."

Ryce said nothing. He moved from pillar to pillar, surveying the walls inch by inch. Matt turned his attention back to the cannon. It pointed upward, right at the center of the stone dome, to the spot where the six ridges converged and the darkness lurked. If the chamber were a silo of sorts, the dome would have to open, wouldn't it? The cannon was immobile; it would shoot the projectile outside, so there had to be some sort of mechanism that expanded the dome.

"Anything?" Matt asked, still looking up and turning the possibility in his head.

"No," Ryce said. "There's only the door that leads to the warhead storage room. There are writings on the floor, though; I still haven't examined them."

"Forget the floor, come here for a second," Matt said. Ryce walked up to him and followed the line of his gaze with his own light, adding to the illumination sweeping across the ceiling. "Do you think we could get it to open?"

Ryce thought about it for a moment. "It's still too high up," he said finally. "How would we get out? Even if we deactivate the suits' graviboots, we can't just jump and float outside. That is, if it does open directly to the moon's surface. It might be the bottom of another bore; we're pretty deep underground."

"If it does open to the surface, climbing out wouldn't be impossible," Matt said, more and more excited by his idea the longer he considered it. It would be a dangerous feat, but at least it would give them a chance to escape. "With the graviboots disabled, the climb would be easier." When Ryce still looked dubious, Matt added, "You wouldn't have to scale the wall. I'll do it, and we'll use a rope to get you up. Frankly, I don't see any other option. We just have to open the roof and see where it leads."

Ryce gave him a long look. Matt could practically see the doubt in his mind. He would be putting his life in Matt's hands, and who was to say that Matt wouldn't simply leave him there once he was in the clear? Given his injury, the chances of him climbing out without assistance were slim. But it was either taking that risk or letting fear block his only chance of escape.

"You're right," he said finally with a sigh. "We have to at least try."

He touched the control panel tentatively. The blocks shifted, but aside from a faint bluish glow, nothing happened. He moved the blocks, searching for a keyhole or anything that resembled an operation switch amid the various etchings. The blocks revealed the cavity with narrow vertical ridges as in the other chamber. "I think this fits the charge," he said. "See, these ridges would fit into the grooves on top of the warhead."

"I'm not trying to fire this thing, just get the roof open," Matt pointed out.

"It looks like the charge also might be the activator," Ryce said, peering closely at the cavity and the writing surrounding it. At least he seemed too preoccupied now to dwell on the pain.

"What? You mean we actually have to fire this thing just to open the silo?" Matt couldn't believe his ears. There was no way he would actually deploy the weapon, uninhabited planet or not. They had no means of making sure they were aiming the cannon in the right direction, and in any case, he didn't want to be anywhere near it when it went off. The equipment was old, they were literally fumbling in the dark with the controls with no idea what they were doing, and accidents were prone to happen.

"Not necessarily, but we do need it to jump-start the system," Ryce said. "The charge has to be inside this depression for the mechanism to work." He fumbled with his kit to take the warhead out.

"Great," Matt muttered. "And what if it closes as soon as you take it out? You'd have to leave it if you want to vamoose out of here."

That gave Ryce pause. He looked at the warhead in his hand.

"You're not actually thinking about it?" Matt said incredulously. "You can either leave it and get out alive or die here cuddling it. Your choice."

Ryce shot him a look. "Would you stop being so melodramatic? I'm simply trying to consider all our options."

"Good to know there are so many of them."

"There could be another charge in there." Ryce nodded toward the narrow door. "We could use that one to activate the system."

"Are you insane?" Matt demanded. "Do you want to be hit by lasers again?"

"Well, now we know about them, so we can be more careful."

"Are you seriously telling me that thing"—Matt pointed at the warhead—"is more important than your life? No amount of money is worth that."

"It's not about the money!" Ryce snapped and had to lean on the platform for support. "I've told you already, this is important. I wouldn't put so much at stake for a bit of cash."

"God, I can't believe someone so smart can also be so damn stupid!" Matt shouted back. "Can't you see you're just being used? What do you think will happen when you take it back to your employer?"

"We can argue about it later," Ryce said, with a touch of desperation. "I just want to see if I can remove the second warhead safely so we can use it. Nothing will happen as long as I don't touch anything."

"You're impossible," Matt said. They were running out of time, and arguing further seemed futile. "Fine, be my guest. Just try not to get killed."

Of course he had to help Ryce open the door and then raise the warhead display pedestal with his infernal laser machine. He wasn't sure what he preferred—for it to be empty, or to find an identical charge. He wasn't comfortable with the thought of there being another one of these things lying around.

The column rose smoothly from the floor, exhibiting the same carved opening. He could see the stand on which the warhead should have rested, but the warhead itself wasn't there. Either it indeed had been used as a test charge on the planet, or it had never been there to begin with, but theirs was the only one now. At least the mayhem in the first chamber hadn't automatically activated an alarm in this room.

Ryce's face fell. Matt could tell he'd been counting on a duplicate charge to use to activate the cannon. Although what he'd have done to avoid triggering the security system while trying to extract it, Matt had no idea. They were lucky, that was all, and he couldn't help but feel relieved.

"Come on, let's get this over with," he said, heading back to the cannon chamber. They'd just have to make do with what they had, and pray it would work.

Ryce trailed after him reluctantly, leaving the door to the tiny chamber open. He paused for a moment, looking up at the long cannon barrel, and then placed the warhead in the cavity very carefully, aligning its ridges with the groves. He grunted as he withdrew his hands. He'd been handling the injury well up until now, but certainly, he couldn't keep it up much longer.

At first nothing happened. Tense seconds passed as they watched the charge unit sitting there inertly. Then, without warning, the groves glowed blue, and the entire "control panel" lit up like a miniature display of Northern Lights.

Matt released the breath he was holding.

"Guess it's been awhile since it was turned on," he remarked. At least nothing was exploding or firing laser beams in all directions.

"If it had ever been turned on at all," Ryce said. He leaned heavily against the plinth, sagging slightly. The bluish light made him look even paler. Matt turned away to look at the blocks.

"Do we have to use the laser again?" he asked.

"I don't think so," Ryce said. "The symbols on the panels are different; there's nothing there to indicate an excitation pattern. They're responding to the touch and our heat signature."

"So how do we know which ones to touch?" Matt asked, eyeing the blocks dubiously. Their situation was not unlike that of a toddler playing with his parents' gadgets, tapping on colorful images with no real understanding of what he was doing. At least that's what it felt like to him. Ryce was probably more at a preschooler level.

"Let me have a closer look," Ryce said, pushing himself up and turning toward the panel.

It proved to be a time-consuming task since the blocks were completely covered in symbols, and Ryce had to sift through them meticulously to find the ones that would trigger the activation sequence. His fingers hovered over the swirling writings as he muttered under his breath, trying to decipher the more complex symbols.

"Don't make it fire," Matt warned, but Ryce ignored him. His ragged breathing and the faint beeping of his suit filled the silence between them, seconds and minutes ticking past like drops of blood from an open wound. It certainly must have felt like it to Ryce, who was having trouble holding himself upright.

"I think I have it," he said finally, turning to Matt.

"Are you sure?"

"About eighty percent sure," Ryce said, deadpan.

Matt snorted. If the activating sequence was wrong, they were probably in for another laser show, but Ryce had to realize that.

"Well, that's better than hundred percent 'don't know,'" he said. "You are absolutely sure it won't fire, though?"

"Yes. The 'fire' option is actually quite clear. See?" Ryce pointed to a large symbol on one of the central blocks that looked like an aggregation of different-sized triangles. To Matt it looked like any other pattern amid the etchings, but if Ryce was sure, he believed him. "As long as we stay away from that one, nothing adverse should happen. Given that the rest of the sequence is correct, of course, but we have no way of knowing until we try."

"It's not like we have any choice, anyway. You ready?"

Ryce nodded. He took a deep steadying breath, shut his eyes briefly, and put his right hand on one of the blocks. Running his fingers over the etched symbols, he then continued on to the next, always picking a precise placement. How he did that after taking just one look at the patterns was a mystery, but Matt had learned not to question Ryce's Onorean cognitive capabilities. He crossed his fingers mentally, studiously following the trail of Ryce's fingertips on the dark blocks.

The sequence was a relatively short one. Ryce had only touched four symbols when the entire panel shifted, and the blocks moved into a new formation. The glow around the charge intensified, and a slight tremor shook the floor of the chamber as some ancient mechanism awoke from its eon-long slumber.

They both looked about in apprehension, their headlamps flashing, ready to bolt at the first sign of trouble. But this time, it wasn't a security system going after intruders. The six columns slowly retracted from their juncture at the top of the dome, sliding down into the floor. The roof panels followed until there was an opening of about fifteen or sixteen feet in diameter above the cannon plinth. This revealed an upper shaft of raw bedrock, which, reaching to about fifty feet high from the floor, was surprisingly not as deep as they'd believed their position below the surface to be.

Above them, beyond its edge, sprawled the infinite darkness of the night sky.

Chapter Twelve

Matt still couldn't believe it had actually worked. He stared at the newly emerged skylight like he couldn't trust it not to disappear. All movement had ceased, though the light around the charge glowed steadily.

"This is it, right?" he asked in a low whisper. He didn't know why he was whispering; it just seemed appropriate for the moment.

"I think so," Ryce said. "As long as we don't touch any more activation symbols. This should hold, at least while the charge is inside. I don't know what will happen when I take it out."

"Okay then," Matt said, assessing the climb. The most difficult part would be scaling the smooth, thirty-feet-high walls of the chamber; the exposed rock beyond offered more purchase. Down here, there was nothing he could hold on to, nothing that offered a foothold or an initial boost.

He touched the wall. He couldn't feel the texture of the stone through his gloves, but it seemed solid, untouched by time. There was no dent or chip to be found on its surface, and he doubted that any of the basic tools he had in his kit would make an impact on it. But then again, they had something far more powerful than a chisel, didn't they? They'd spent their entire duration here using it.

"Do you think that laser of yours can do some damage to the walls?"

"If it's regular stone and not some superstrong alloy I previously haven't heard of, I don't see why not," Ryce said. He sat down gingerly at the base of the plinth, leaning back against it. He must have been utterly exhausted by now. "Crank up the intensity a bit, and use a direct beam, no coordinates."

Despite Matt's reluctance to handle the laser, it was solely up to him at this point. The beam cut into the stone like a knife, raising a cloud of dust and small shards. The process was slower than he would have liked, but Matt wasn't aiming to carve out actual steps, just make a few gouges deep enough to hold on to. With the gravipull function turned off, he'd be buoyant, his weight significantly reduced in the weak local gravity field, so the effort of climbing wouldn't be as strenuous as it would have been in other circumstances.

It felt like time had slowed down, but he just kept going, working as methodically as he could, though at some point his hands began to ache from holding the device steady. Gouge after gouge, each only about an inch wide, appeared on the wall, going up to the edge, where the artificial smoothness met the rough texture of the rock.

"Well, there's that," he said once he judged the work was finished. His helmet light picked up every detail as he eyed the wall critically, its pristine slick surface now marred with ugly, uneven scars that looked almost obscene against the austere backdrop of the rest of the structure. But Matt's reverence toward Mnirian legacy had diminished somewhat over the last hours. Ingenious or not, these creatures had purposefully developed something intended to exterminate life on an overwhelming scale. Matt was not going to feel guilty over scratching their shiny pretty wall.

He packed as much as he could in his kit, leaving the laser generator with Ryce, in case he might need it again. Please, just let this work, he prayed silently. Let the roof stay open long enough for both of us to get out.

"Hold on, you hear?" he said, and Ryce only nodded.

Matt disabled the gravipull function in his boots, went up to the scorched wall, and gave his tired fingers and arms a good shake, gearing up for the long climb. Now, he needed to focus again for one last push. He gripped the first gouge, braced his foot against the wall and hauled himself up, propelled by the sudden feeling of near-weightlessness.

Even so, the first few feet were the most difficult. He managed to get a good grip with his gloves, but because of inertia, he risked pushing himself away from the wall with nearly every move. After a while, he got into the hang of it, grabbing at the gouges and pulling himself up carefully while gaining purchase with his feet, keeping his movements small and precise. It was stressful to say the least, and he wished he'd spent a little more time letting himself adjust to this new condition. The sound of his labored breathing filled his ears, and he tried very hard not to look down. He almost slipped once or twice, his heart nearly dropping to his stomach each time, but somehow he managed not to fall to the floor. Even if such a dive wouldn't result in serious injury, it would mean he'd have to start all over again, and he could really do without a repeat performance. Slowly, inch by inch, foot by foot, he crawled upward, toward the open sky.

He didn't know quite how much time it took him to make the climb, but it couldn't have been more than twenty minutes until he finally reached the point where the edge of the wall chamber met the bedrock. It stretched upward for another twenty feet and then slanted gently away from the opening.

The exposed rock proved more difficult a challenge. Its texture was rough, but not nearly enough to provide a good grip. Don't think about falling, Matt told himself, plodding slowly on. Don't think about it. At this height, he risked breaking a limb or worse, and that would be it for the both of them.

Just a little bit further, just a few more minutes…and the tilt of the wall changed. He climbed onto a flat surface, and for a minute just lay there, facedown, luxuriating in his success.

When at last he caught his breath, he sat up cautiously, making sure to move away from the edge. The vent he'd just climbed opened to the bottom of a large crater. The asteroid belt, slowly spinning around them, was like a thick scattering of tiny holes punched into a black velvet curtain, rendering the distant outline of the planet muted in comparison. It was the most desolate place imaginable, but he'd never been so happy to see open space in his life.

Thankfully the walls of the crater weren't very steep, so getting out wouldn't present a problem. Out here the suit's scanners picked up the location of the shuttle. They hadn't strayed too far afield, but they still had some way to go.

Matt sifted through the tools in his kit until he found a retractable rope—a compact spool of woven silicon-coated wire cord—and fastened it around the biggest boulder he could find in the immediate vicinity. The length of it would come a bit short of the floor, but that was okay—Ryce was tall enough to reach it. He crawled to the edge of the opening, peering inside with the help of his helmet light. He had to switch it to high beam to see all the way to the bottom. It was draining the battery, but it wasn't what concerned him at this point. The barrel of the cannon came just short of the opening, and Ryce was huddled below. He didn't lift his head even when the pool of light touched him.

"Hey," Mat said, raising his voice just a bit over the internal comm channel. Shit, if Ryce picked this time to pass out… "Can you hear me?"

"Yes," Ryce said. He finally looked up, squinting at the light.

"Good," Matt said, more than a little relieved. He didn't want to consider the possibility of climbing back down and attempting to haul himself up with an unconscious Ryce strapped to his back.

"I'll take the charge out now and see what happens." The circle of light followed Ryce as he struggled back to his feet and ran a hand over the control panel blocks. The glow rippled, but nothing changed. Matt held his breath as he watched him reach inside and remove the charge, painstakingly slowly, though his instinct must have screamed at him to yank it out as fast as he could. He was half-expecting the roof sections to snap back together like a set of jaws.

But nothing happened. The control panel still glowed eerily, and the vent opening stayed as it was. Now it was time to move quickly, before the mechanism could revert back without the activator unit.

"I'm lowering the rope."

Ryce stuffed the warhead and the laser generator in his bag. Matt wasn't comfortable with the thought of the weapon being jostled around on the way, but it couldn't be helped. Ryce grabbed the end of the rope once it was within reach and hooked it to his utility belt.

"I'm ready," he said.

Matt took hold of the rope and pulled. The newly reactivated graviboots now kept him firmly lodged in place. Ryce, with his own weight now significantly reduced, was pushing himself off the wall instead of just hanging on to the rope. But since he was only using one arm and protecting the other from bumping into the wall with each bounce, his climb was encumbered and still required effort on Matt's part.

At last Ryce's head popped out of the vent, and Matt hastened to pull him out by the shoulders. Once on solid ground, Ryce curled up, cradling his injured hand. His breathing was coming out in sobs. Matt crouched beside him and patted him on the shoulder.

"Rest a bit," he said. "You did it. The shuttle isn't far."

It was nothing short of incredible that they'd made it out in the end—a mix of quick thinking and blind luck that had kept them alive and relatively whole through the ordeal. They were still not safely back, but they'd managed to avoid dying in an underground tomb, and had completed the mission for Matt's client.

He took the bag containing the warhead from Ryce and strapped it to his belt. The question now was, what were they going to do with it? Now that Matt knew what it was, he couldn't ignore the implications of putting a weapon of this kind in any individual's hands. He wouldn't even place this kind of power in the hands of the Federation, not even for the ostensible purpose of countering the Alraki threat. No matter what Ryce believed about his employer's noble intentions, Matt was a better judge of human nature, and his experience had taught him it rarely lived up to its professed virtues. Even those who started off as idealists fell victims to the allure of power and money more often than not. And being capable of wiping out a planet's entire population with a flip of a switch was entirely too much power.

Usually Matt couldn't afford having an oversensitive conscience. He couldn't afford it now, when a hundred thousand creds were at stake, some of which he'd already spent. There was no way for him to stay afloat while indebted to the mysterious Mr. Ari and Pat Gentry. He'd have to sell *Lady Lisa* just to get out of trouble, and if he did that, it would be the end. The end of freedom, the end of his little dysfunctional family, the end of the life he'd managed to carve for himself. He couldn't fuck this job up, not now when they'd gotten what they came for.

Ryce moaned and sat up, shaking his head a bit.

"You okay?"

"Yeah," Ryce said.

"Good. Nothing worse than dying a virgin."

For one tense moment he thought he'd said the wrong thing, but then Ryce barked a laugh.

"Let's get back to the shuttle," he said. "I'm dying to get out of this suit."

Matt helped him up, offering a shoulder for him to lean on. The ground was rough and uneven, mottled with cracks and fissures, but nothing deep enough to present a real danger. As shallow as the crater was, its wall was a much more serious hurdle. Stone debris, rubble, and dust had accumulated there, creating a sort of ramp for them to climb, and they once again forwent the familiarity of 1 g gravity pull for the easiness of simply leaping above the obstacles in their path. Ryce stumbled on first with Matt bringing up the rear, ready to catch him if he slipped. They didn't stop to rest when they reached the upper ground, choosing instead to plow on, once again clinging to each other to keep true to course, under their new buoyancy.

Matt could have sworn the last few hundred yards to the shuttle were the most vexatious he'd ever had to walk, but the most uplifting as well. He'd never been happier in his life to see that shoddy little piece of spacecraft. It was clearly visible against the flat terrain and the blackness of the sky, and its beacon wouldn't have let them stray in any case.

Matt literally pushed Ryce up the ramp when the hatch opened. They stumbled into the pressure chamber, barely waiting for the hatch to slide closed and the inner door to open before tearing away their helmets.

"I'm never going on a field trip with you again," Matt said, leaning back on the wall and closing his eyes for a moment. The brightly lit, crammed interior of the shuttle's entryway was comfortingly familiar after the eerie darkness of the alien base. He put the helmet back in its wall compartment in the narrow corridor and undid the fastenings of the suit. It felt like shedding a cocoon and emerging subtly transformed, both enlightened and burdened by his experience.

"Believe me, I'm not planning on doing it either." Ryce shuffled down the corridor and sat heavily in one of the passenger seats before starting to take off his own suit. His hands were shaking.

"Here, let me," Matt said, coming to help. This was not how he'd fantasized about undressing Ryce. He had to admit the man looked good even wearing nothing but a crumpled T-shirt and underwear, his body strong and lean though hunched with fatigue. They both needed a shower and a change of clothes, but given the situation, that could wait till they got back to the ship.

Ryce grimaced as he took off the gloves. His left hand was swollen and trembled when he tried to flex his fingers. A little above the wrist there was a neat little hole, going all the way through. Its edges were burned and the flesh around it was red and hot to the touch. Matt poked it gingerly to check if a temporary splint was needed. It didn't look like the laser had cut through the bones, but he was no expert. Tony was the one who usually handled any kind of injury. Granted, her medical knowledge was mostly theoretical, but she'd gained some practical experience in her four years of lugging about on the Lisa, tending various cuts and bruises. He just hoped his skills were enough to treat the wound until she could take a look.

What worried him even more was the fact that they still had to make it back to *Lady Lisa* through the asteroid field, and they couldn't afford having Ryce distracted by pain or unable to steer, since he was so adamant about using manual flight control.

Ryce's suit was a throwaway, but Matt stowed it neatly anyway. Val could probably salvage some parts of it at least. He took out a first aid kit and set to work on cleaning the wound. There was almost no blood, but he used an antiseptic anyway and covered the puncture with some colloid tape. He applied anti-inflammatory cream on the surrounding exposed skin as an afterthought and bandaged it up. Thankfully there were analgesics in the kit as well, and Ryce took them docilely. There was also a hypodermic syringe with stimulants, but Matt left that alone; simple painkillers would suffice for now. It was a measure of how bad Ryce was feeling that he let Matt take the lead on the ministrations without question or a single acerbic comment.

"You have the weapon, right?" was all he asked when they were finished. He closed his eyes and leaned back in his seat, waiting for the painkillers to take effect.

"Right here," Matt said and patted the bag, which he had carefully set aside. "But I won't let you have it."

Chapter Thirteen

Ryce sat up sharply.

"What?"

"Not until you tell me exactly who this Mr. Ari is and what he wants the weapon for," Matt said.

He'd had time to reflect on this during their miserable journey to the shuttle. Confronting Ryce, and by extension, his paying client, regarding the weapon was doubtless the wrong decision, for so many reasons. He'd already ruined his life once by doing what he thought was right when he'd quit the Fleet so abruptly, defying everything his parents believed in, and he was probably doing it again right now. But how could he live with himself if something horrible happened, and he could have prevented it? Wasn't that the reason he was so bitterly disillusioned with the military, that they allowed such things to take place as long as it served their agenda? At the very least, Ryce owed him an explanation. He refused to be a mindless tool in somebody else's hands. Maybe this time he'd have to forgo both the job and the pay.

"That wasn't the deal," Ryce said in a low voice.

"Yeah, well, I'm changing the deal. If you're not happy about it, you're welcome to go down there again and see if you can find another one of those warheads stashed around somewhere."

Ryce glared at him. "I don't do well with ultimatums."

"I bet you don't do well with being shot through the arm for pawing precious artifacts either, but you don't have much choice in the matter, do you?" In the face of Ryce's offended silence, he added, "Come on, you knew what it was. What was the plan? Use me and my crew to get the weapon without drawing too much attention to yourself, and then off us to keep it quiet?"

"Of course not!" Ryce said indignantly. He looked genuinely appalled by the suggestion. But of course Matt knew him well enough by now to know he was not comfortable playing dirty. His employer, on the other hand, might not be telling his young, impressionable proxy the entire truth regarding his intentions—like murder or potential genocide.

"Then what? Why is it so damn important to you?"

Ryce sighed and slumped back in his seat. He was silent for a few moments and then said: "If I tell you, you must keep it confidential, for both our sakes. If this gets out…"

"Confidential is my middle name."

Ryce looked unconvinced but leaned back again, cradling his wounded arm.

"It will come as no surprise to you that 'Ari' is a pseudonym. I'm acting on behalf of my former commander, Commodore James Archer. I served under him during my first duty assignment on the *Nikosia*, and I got to know him better on one of our deep-space rounds. He gave me a letter of commendation for getting my squadron out of crossfire." Ryce glanced at him uncertainly, but as Matt didn't challenge him, continued.

"He was a senior officer, so we couldn't exactly be friends, but we spoke together a great deal. It turned out we had common interests aside from our careers. He is a xenohistory buff like myself, and he wanted to know more about my Onorean origins. It was so nice to finally talk to someone who understood me, and what I was about, who didn't see me as a tight-ass upstart, like the other pilots. Even back home, there had been no one with whom I could have an intelligent conversation that didn't revolve around types of ore. He thought we were very much alike, that I had potential to follow in his footsteps in regard to a military career."

Matt nodded as Ryce paused, caught up in his recollections. It all made sense—Ryce's connection to the man, his deference and willingness to risk his career for an obscure cause. Truth be told, he was a little surprised Ryce had decided to confide in him, since Matt's leverage was tenuous at best. Maybe, given all they'd been through, he'd earned a measure of the man's trust. And Matt had learned something about the young pilot that continued to attract him. Somewhere along the line, Ryce's opinion of him had become important.

Clearly, Ryce's opinion of this Commodore Archer was pretty high. It was understandable that he'd been a bit star-struck, drawing the attention of a well-known and respected commander, all the more if there was an intellectual camaraderie between them.

"That was over a year ago," Ryce went on. "There was a great deal of trouble with the Alraki at that time, especially in the Salua sector, where the *Nikosia* was stationed. Now things are quieter, but then it looked like a full-blown war was about to break out. Commodore Archer was advocating for a preemptive strike on the Alraki base in the neighboring system. He'd lost an entire ship at the Battle of Gunnar about five years ago, while commanding the twenty-first Flotilla, and he didn't want that to happen at Salua."

"I heard about that," Matt said. He vaguely remembered seeing reports and pictures about one of the rare times the Alraki dared to engage the human Fleet in a large-scale confrontation. It had been a major victory for the humans, but it was dearly bought. Thousands of lives had been lost during the course of a few hours. It happened just after he'd quit, and he remembered being glad about not having to deal with the fallout of that particular fiasco. "Didn't this Archer get a Band of Courage for winning that battle?"

"He did," Ryce said. "But he wished things had gone differently then. He wanted to act first, so there wouldn't be another Gunnar, but the Central Command was against his idea. They thought it would only provoke further escalation. But I happened to agree with him.

"I lost my parents and close to everybody I've known since I was a child in an Alraki raid. The Fleet isn't big enough to protect every colony, every station, every ship, and that's what they're counting on. They're like vultures, going for the isolated prey. But if we force them into a defensive position..."

Ryce shook his head, glancing at Matt and taking a moment to calm himself. "Anyway, his plan was rejected. And then he told me about something he'd seen once, in a Mnirian site excavation on the moon of Greta-7. He said it was a diagram on a wall fragment, depicting star coordinates. The writing around it was only partly preserved, but he was able to piece it together, albeit crudely. It was a mention of a planetary-scale weapon. He showed me the pictures, and together we were able to figure out what it was. The coordinates led us to the Colanta system, and to this moon. I thought it was a long shot, but Commodore Archer insisted we try to find it, and he was right.

"R & D was working on a laser generator designed to be used as a handheld unlocking device at Mnirian sites—like you've said, a miniature version of the spacecraft-mounted jumpgate activation equipment—and Archer managed to secure a working prototype for me to study and take along, since we'd have no other means of getting inside a sealed structure."

"If he's such a big shot in the Fleet, how come he's hiring a smuggler?" Here's what Matt really wanted to know: Why was Archer risking his protégé's reputation by making him do his dirty work? But Ryce would undoubtedly resent his phrasing.

"Like I said, it was a long shot." Ryce shrugged. "We had no solid way of confirming if our attempts at translation were correct, that it was indeed a serviceable weapon. It was most likely that whatever the Mnirians had built here would have been destroyed long ago."

"And he wanted to keep it under wraps," Matt interjected. "And if the weapon proved serviceable, he'd use it for…what? He'd really go against CenCom's orders for the pleasure of wiping out that Alraki base?"

"No. He's looking at the larger picture. Destroying a single outpost here and there won't change anything in the grand scheme of things, not on a galactic scale. But a weapon of this magnitude is a tiebreaker. A threat like that would force the Alraki to agree to a nonaggression pact, ending the war altogether."

Matt raised an eyebrow. "Ending the war with a threat of some ancient alien weapon that nobody has ever heard of or was able to construct independently? That's a preposterous assumption. I would laugh in his face if he came to me with such an ultimatum, and I'm a lot more reasonable that the average Alraki."

"But it exists," Ryce pointed out stubbornly. "We saw ourselves that all the systems at the base were fully operational, despite their age and disuse. There is no reason to presume that the warhead itself is not functional as well. Like I said, a cannon is a rather simple piece of machinery; there would be no difficulty in building one specifically for this charge, or, alternatively, transporting one of the original Mnirian cannons off the Colanta moon."

"It's nothing more than pure conjecture. The Alraki are not timid children; you can't scare them with stories of mythical doomsday devices. To get them even listening to a negotiation proposal, Archer would have to prove that it actually works. He'd have to demonstrate it. On a base, or an outpost, or even a planet. And then he'd have to be very good at poker, because he'd have only one of these warheads, and if that little fact leaked out, there would be hell to pay."

"Those are just details," Ryce retorted. "The important thing is we have this weapon in our hands. The strategy around it can be sorted out after we get it back safely. The warhead technology could potentially be replicated, once R & D takes a closer look at it. It could at least get us a truce, an uneasy one for sure, but there would be no more senseless bloodshed, no more raids against distant settlements. This threat would keep the Alraki at bay."

Matt huffed in disapproval. He, on the other hand, thought that those details were pretty damn important, and they didn't add up. Not to mention there was no way Fleet brass would approve such a crazy, half-assed plan. Whatever Archer's endgame was, Matt was willing to bet his precious *Lisa* that nobody in Fleet Central Command was in on it. Come to think of it, there was only one possible way to end the war with the Alraki with only one doomsday device available. And that was using it directly against the enemy home world.

Ryce couldn't see it, of course, being too noble-minded to consider such an option or suspect his beloved commander capable of such atrocity. Matt was willing to bet Archer hadn't revealed his true plans to Ryce. And Ryce was too smitten with his father figure of a commander to critically analyze the promises he was being fed, and which he was now spewing back. Couldn't he see that no man, not even the most virtuous one in existence (which he suspected wasn't the case here, war hero or not), should hold that much power over others?

But whether Archer was going rogue or had some top-secret black-ops scheme in the works, it was also likely he wasn't planning on letting Matt and his crew run loose with potentially damaging information. No wonder he hadn't balked at the price; dead men didn't have to be paid. What his intentions were in regard to Ryce was anyone's guess, but Matt was not buying that "taking a young prodigy under his wing" crap. Jaded worldview or not, nobody piled on so much nonsense without an ulterior motive.

Ryce, who undoubtedly sensed Matt's reservations, said: "I should report to Archer that we've found it."

It was probably an attempt to prevent Matt from getting rid of the thing. He hadn't considered yet what he should do. Ryce's story only served to further complicate the situation, which was precarious enough already.

"Let's wait till we get back on the ship," he said in a lighter tone. "We're not out of the woods yet. You wouldn't want to get Archer's hopes up before crashing into an asteroid, would you?"

"Encouraging as always," Ryce said and pushed himself out of the chair. "As fetching as you look in those shorts, we should probably change and see to getting ourselves out of the woods, as you put it."

"So you did notice my shorts!" Matt followed him with his gaze, taking the opportunity to ogle the man's backside as he left the cabin.

☆☆☆

He gave Ryce some privacy to change back into his fatigues and went to check on the control panel. Unsurprisingly, all the scanner readings were normal, the indicator lights bleeping sedately. It seemed like they'd spent an eternity wandering the halls and tunnels of the long-forgotten complex and dragging themselves back over the rough terrain, but in reality, it had been no more than ten hours since they'd entered the cave. The suits had provided them with enough distilled fluids, but Matt was decidedly hungry now that all other immediate needs had been taken care of. There were some dried rations stowed in the overhead compartments, along with thermal blankets and other emergency equipment. He could definitely go for some protein bars right now. Even the prospect of Tony's famous canned tomato soup was enough to make his mouth water.

After Ryce was done, it was his turn to put on clean clothes and freshen up as best he could. It would have been better to rest a little longer before heading on the journey back, but Matt was loath to stay even a minute longer than necessary in this place.

"All set?" he asked, joining Ryce in the cockpit.

The other man nodded. He looked marginally better now, the color returning to his cheeks, but his left hand was in a makeshift sling. Matt frowned when he saw it.

"Are you sure you're up to it?"

"Do we have a choice?" Ryce countered.

The control panel suddenly lit up before he had the chance to activate his adapters, and Tony's urgent voice came through loud and clear over the external channel. "Captain, we have a situation here."

Matt exchanged a look with Ryce.

"What kind of a situation?"

"There's an incoming ship at the jumpgate."

"What?"

How was that even possible? They were in the proverbial middle of nowhere. It was just a name on a star map. There was a reason nobody had taken interest in the place for millennia, and all of a sudden it was the damn Sawyer Strait.

Then a thought hit him. What if it was the Feds? What if Ryce's employer had come to finish the job? Or worse, what if their little plan had been discovered by Fleet CenCom, and now they were swooping in to arrest them and claim the prize? He glared at Ryce.

"Did you send out a transmission?"

Ryce shook his head. The confused look on the other man's face was genuine. He wasn't expecting anyone either. Though of course he could just be a disposable pawn, with no knowledge of the larger scheme. For all his brains, Ryce was naive enough to be fooled, that much was clear already.

Matt plopped into the pilot seat, while Ryce took the second chair. They were not going anywhere until they knew what they were up against.

"Is it a Federation vessel?" he asked. Realistically, who else could it be? He grimaced as he imagined the long list of indictments he and his crew could be facing. And that was, of course, the lesser of two evils, since the alternative was being murdered in cold blood by a goal-oriented military officer intent on keeping his game plan secret.

"No." There was some static and background noise, and then Tony said: "The ship's unmarked, and I can't get a reading, but it's definitely armed. Captain... I think it's pirates."

Chapter Fourteen

"Shit," Matt whispered. Just when the situation couldn't get any worse. "Shit."

"I haven't heard of a pirate base in this sector." Ryce frowned. "Though an orphan jumpgate would present a convenient stomping ground."

"Or maybe somebody tipped them off about your oh-so-secret bunker location," Matt said, fighting the urge to laugh hysterically at Ryce's puzzlement. It didn't really matter if they'd accidentally stumbled into a pirates' den, or if the newcomers were the competition Archer had been concerned about. The only thing that mattered was that they had to get the hell out of here. Now.

"Captain, they're hailing us," Tony said.

So much for trying to slip away unnoticed. "Transmit on-screen," Matt said. Ryce turned his chair away from the window bay, probably to avoid being seen, but his tense profile indicated he was listening intently.

The screen lit up, displaying the dimly lit interior of the other ship's bridge. The man occupying the captain's chair was broad and rough looking, with dark matted hair and beard and an electronic patch over his right eye.

"Spears," the man said in a deep voice.

Matt dug his fingers into the armrests to the point of pain, forgetting all about Ryce, Archer, Mnirian superweapons, and everything else. It was as if the world had suddenly crashed and the pieces had rearranged themselves into a scene from one of his nightmares. Maybe he was hallucinating. Maybe he was still lying on the floor of an underground tunnel, having lucid dreams in the darkness while slowly running out of oxygen. Somehow it would have been better if he were.

It was surprising how calm his voice sounded when he replied.

"Rodgers. How did you know where to find me?"

"You should thank your old chum Pat Gentry. Apparently he has a few friends at Freeport control, and one hell of a grudge against you. It seems you have a special talent for pissing off the wrong people."

Pat, you fucking son of a bitch, Matt thought wearily. That was the trouble with getting mixed up with violent psychopaths; it was all fun and games until they turned on you over some hogwash.

"I've got your precious tin can in my sights," Rodgers continued. "Give me one good reason why I shouldn't blow you out of the sky right now."

"No! No. I'm not on board. I'm on a shuttle, planetside." Begging probably wasn't the best tactic to use here, but seeing Dylan Rodgers face-to-face threw him off completely. "You have no bone to pick with my crew. I'm the one you want. Just let them go."

One of Rodgers' crew members came up to him and whispered something in his ear. Rodgers nodded and turned to Matt again.

"Tell you what, Spears. I don't give a fuck about your crew, but they ain't going nowhere until you get your ass here in that shuttle. I know they're listening in, so nobody better try anything funny, or I'll open fire. There's nowhere to go, unless I let them out."

"Fine," Matt said hastily. "I'll come. Just…don't do anything, okay?"

"You've got an hour, Spears," Rodgers said. "You should remember I'm not very patient."

The transmission disconnected, leaving behind a heavy, sticky silence, interrupted only by the sound of Ryce turning back in his chair. Matt exhaled softly, and then punched the control panel in frustration.

"Captain," Tony said with urgency. "What should we do? I can try making a run for it, send a distress call to the nearest station—"

"No!" Matt steeled himself for the impending exchange. The last thing he needed right now was for his crew to take initiative and make the wrong move with Rodgers watching. "No. Don't try anything, and no calls. Stay put. I'm going to Rodgers."

"You're shitting me," Tony said after a leaden pause, her voice dangerously calm. "Matt, tell me you're shitting me."

"Sorry to disappoint you, hot stuff," he said. "But I have a plan. Just promise me you'll skedaddle at the first sign of trouble. Get to that jumpgate no matter what. Hopefully, I'll be joining you soon, but if not, don't wait, just get the hell out."

She proceeded to tell him exactly what she thought of his planning skills in a manner that was decidedly inappropriate for a subordinate. Matt waited patiently till she ran out of breath and then said:

"I'd love to keep chatting, but I'm afraid Mr. Faine's delicate sensibilities"—Matt tossed him a quick look—"would be offended, leaving him too flustered to steer properly." And then he added in a serious tone, "Really, Tony, I'll be fine. Tell Val to take it easy, and look after my *Lisa*." He disconnected before she could protest, and rubbed the bridge of his nose tiredly.

"She does love you a lot," Ryce observed.

"I guess that's why my ears are still burning," Matt said. But Ryce was right. He'd come to think of Tony and Val as his little adopted family. They all had a past, something that they were running from, and that was what held them together. He pretended not to have any regrets, but now he regretted not having the chance to see them one last time and say good-bye to his ship. He just had to make sure they got away safely.

He wished there was a way to get Ryce away safely, too. Matt had first-hand experience of what awaited them with Rodgers. Captives provided a certain type of fresh entertainment for the crew. What Rodgers would do to him, considering the man had a personal grudge, was too terrifying to contemplate. Matt needed to stay alert and not let himself dwell on the possibilities.

"I have to agree with Tony, though," Ryce said, leaning toward him. "You can't be serious about giving yourself up to this guy. Who is he, anyway, and what does he want with you?"

Matt really didn't want to go into it right now. Talking about it just made it worse. But that wouldn't be fair to Ryce, who was now caught up in the middle of it. He deserved to know what was going on. Matt slumped in his seat and rubbed his face tiredly.

"When I left Fleet, I was basically drifting—taking odd jobs, working for other runners and freight haulers. I had already been working as a navigator for the North Star Company for a while, transporting crude oil they were drilling on Lea-4, when we were attacked. They captured the ship and the entire crew, and I…" He swallowed. "I tried to get away on my own. I mean, I barely knew any of those people, and I had a better chance if…" He stopped. He was making excuses, and it was pathetic. He took a deep breath and continued, "I didn't make it. This guy, Rodgers, wasn't happy about having to chase me. They like clean jobs, no loose ends, you know? If it's just the cargo they're after, they herd all the prisoners into the airlock and open the hatch."

He fell silent, fiddling with the armrest. There was a small hole in the beige polyurethane upholstery, and he picked at it. It was easier to concentrate on that than on what he would read on his companion's face.

"What happened?" Ryce asked quietly.

"That's exactly what happened. To most of the others, I mean. As for me... There was lots of bad shit we don't have time to get into right now. At least I was still alive, though." He didn't need to recall the nightmares of those few days. There were plenty of new nightmares waiting for him in a short while anyway. "But I did manage to escape finally, and I ended up injuring him in the process."

"You did?"

"Yeah. Why do you think he has the patch?" The hole was bigger than his thumb now, and he left it alone, wiping his palms on his pants. "He's got it in for me. I thought I was safe in Sonora; it's always teeming with the Feds, and pirates rarely operate there. So much for that, huh?"

Ryce touched his hand, forcing Matt to look up at him. There was no pity or revulsion in his eyes, only concern.

"Matt, listen to me. He murdered all those people, not you. It wasn't your fault, and you can't blame yourself for what happened. I get it that you feel guilty for running instead of staying and trying to help. I don't know if you could have changed anything or not. All I know is that you can't change it now." He gripped Matt's hand hard. "You're a different person now. You could have left me in that silo to die, and run off with something that is beyond priceless, but you didn't. You could stay here, safely hidden in this asteroid field, where Rodgers can't find you, and sacrifice your friends, but you won't. For what it's worth, I was wrong about you. You have courage, and you have a heart. And I can't—I won't—let you run to him blindly. He'll kill you."

"I know." It wasn't easy to say. Looking into those gray eyes, all Matt could think of was how much he wanted to live. Ryce was arrogant, stubborn, and green around the edges, but he was a pure soul. And if Ryce believed in him, then he could believe in himself too. "But I have to do something. There's no way in hell I'm gonna let him hurt my crew. Or you, for that matter."

Matt sat up straight. They were running out of time, and he couldn't risk crossing Rodgers when so much was at stake. "First, we have to get through the minefield."

"Wait, you don't actually believe he'll just let your ship go," Ryce said incredulously. "You said so yourself, they don't want any loose ends, especially when a personal vendetta is involved. Even if you turn yourself in, he'll hunt your crew down."

"Do you have a better idea?" Matt asked. "We're stuck in the middle of nowhere, and they're blocking our only escape route. Maybe if I offer him something, he'll be willing to cut a deal."

"Like what?" Ryce asked, and then his expression changed. "You're not thinking about offering him the weapon. If it falls into the wrong hands…"

"Of course I'm not offering him the weapon!" The shock, the pressure and the helplessness—it was all building up rapidly, and Matt turned to him fiercely. "What do you take me for?"

He should have known Ryce didn't really think any better of him. Anyway, there wasn't any time left for disappointment or recrimination. They had to act quickly if he wanted to get everybody out of this mess, preferably himself included. First things first. He stood up.

"You're up. Try not to crash us on the way back; that'll put Rodgers in a real shitty mood. And don't worry, your precious weapon is as safe as can be."

Ryce pressed his lips into a hard line and sat down in the vacated pilot chair, activating his adapters with a quick touch.

"What makes you think he'll negotiate with you?"

In all honesty, Matt believed there was a better chance to successfully negotiate with the Alraki than with Rodgers. But not having a clear plan in mind, his only option seemed to be to stall for time until something came to him. He wasn't about to get into it with Ryce, though. The man apparently already thought he was willing to do anything to save his own hide, and it would be a waste of time to convince him otherwise. Admitting to him that he was improvising as he went along wouldn't help either.

"Wipe out the shuttle log, all of it," he told Ryce. At least Rodgers wouldn't be able to glean the exact location of the Mnirian base from the computer.

He was tempted to leave the warhead right here on the moon, stashing it somewhere, but thought better of it. There simply was no time. Taking it back with them would be a huge risk, but he was counting on none of the pirates figuring out what the thing was, even if they did found it. With nothing to discharge or detonate it, the warhead would be just a harmless curiosity.

He cast about for a place to stash it, leaving Ryce to interface with the computer. Unfortunately, the tiny shuttle didn't offer a lot of hiding places, certainly none that would be inconspicuous. Finally, he stowed the warhead in the backpack of one of the unused space suits, together with the laser generator. It seemed like a good idea to keep them together at this point, and it wasn't a place anybody would suspect of hiding weapons.

"Ready?" he asked as he returned to the cockpit. Precious minutes were ticking away. It had taken them longer than an hour to get to the moon, when Ryce was on the top of his game; traversing the mine-riddled expanse would now require a superhuman effort.

Ryce hesitated, and Matt's guts churned. If he couldn't do it, they were as good as dead, and Tony and Val would soon be dead too.

"If you're not—" he began in a sinking voice.

"Get me the stimulants from the first aid kit," Ryce said tersely, cutting him off.

Matt wasted no time in asking if he was sure. If ever there was time for drastic measures, this was it. He fetched the syringe and helped Ryce roll up his sleeve, wincing as he plunged the needle into his forearm.

"Okay," Ryce said, cool and collected once again. His left hand was encased in its sling, but he gripped the control stick confidently with his right. Matt strapped himself into the copilot seat, monitoring the on-screen data feed. The shuttle shuddered as the thrusters kicked in, and they took off in a graceful arc, soaring into the sky and leaving the wretched place behind.

As the shuttle wove its way around the moon, a small asteroid bumped into the spacecraft, making them both jump.

"Sorry," Ryce said. He veered the shuttle around a larger boulder that was spinning at them from the port side.

"I'm sorry too," Matt told him, not looking at him. "If there was any way to keep you out of this…"

But there wasn't. Whatever the outcome, Ryce was stuck with him, and this time it was Matt's fault.

"I know." Ryce glanced at him quickly and turned his attention back to the cluttered stretch of space before them. He held the control stick loosely, guiding it with gentle motions, his eyes intent on the screen. The shuttle glided among the debris at a much greater speed than either of them would have been comfortable with under different circumstances, but so far, Ryce managed to avoid any further collisions.

A tense silence settled between them. Mat knew it was his responsibility to see all of them out of this mess. This wasn't something he could run from, even if it felt as though the enormity of the task would crush him.

The trouble was, he didn't know what to do. As the initial panic receded, he wracked his brain for a course of action that wouldn't end in Rodgers killing them and blowing up his ship, but there was nothing. The two of them couldn't fight Rodgers' entire crew, just as the defenseless *Lady Lisa* couldn't take on the pirate ship. And Rodgers was not the kind of guy to forgo settling a score for some vague reason. Besides, Rodgers had a number of surefire methods of making them talk at his disposal. There would be no deal; he would torture them until they would be only too eager to spill everything they knew about the base, if they were to mention it. Matt remembered his earlier careless remark to Ryce, wishing he'd kept his mouth shut. There were definitely worse things than dying a virgin, not the least of them, dying after forcibly losing said virginity.

Think, he told himself as the rubble floated past the window screen. This couldn't be it. Surely there was something he could do to extricate them from this mess. Charm might be useless, but he still had his wits. And God, did he need a drink right now. He thought longingly of his stashed whiskey that might as well have been a thousand light-years away.

The shuttle jounced gently from another shallow hit, and Ryce cursed softly under his breath, shaking Matt out of his preoccupation.

"We have barely ten minutes left," he said, taking a look at the time flashing on the bottom of the screen.

"We'll be there," Ryce said curtly. The shuttle picked up speed, and the debris seemed to hurtle straight at them. Matt fidgeted in his seat, tensing in anticipation of a hit with each passing asteroid.

So it was that the exit out of the asteroid field took him a little by surprise; it was like coming out of a dense thicket into a clearing. The shuttle slipped into higher orbit, skirting just along the edge of the rocky belt. Colanta-3 turned slowly beneath them, but their attention was on the lone jumpgate, tinged bloodred against the black backdrop, and the spaceship that waited there. Matt let out a long, nervous breath and felt Ryce relax imperceptibly beside him. They had made it out alive and whole, but now they were facing an even greater danger—one that Ryce couldn't overcome with his quick mind and honed reflexes alone.

Out of the pot and into the fire they went.

Chapter Fifteen

"There," Ryce said, locking on the coordinates and bringing an enlarged image on-screen.

Rodgers' starship, a TH-class heavy raider, appeared in no official registry of any sector, but Matt knew it went by the name of *Black Baza*. Like all ships of its class, it was robust and packed considerable speed and firepower. It was a formidable sight, but Matt couldn't tear his gaze away, his mouth suddenly dry. He'd hoped never to see this particular ship again. He didn't want to remember anything about it.

It hovered just outside the jumpgate, effectively cutting off any chance of escape. Of course, the shuttlecraft didn't have any jump-activating capability, and Matt wouldn't make some mad dash for freedom, leaving *Lady Lisa* to fend for herself anyway. He hoped if push came to shove, Tony would find some way to reach the jumpgate on her own. His *Lisa* was outside visible range now, drifting along the planet's outer orbit.

The ship grew larger and larger on-screen as they approached, until there was nothing else but its dark hull.

Ryce threw Matt a sideways look.

"Are you sure you want to do this?"

"I haven't been less sure of anything my entire life," Matt said wearily. "Just stay on course."

The bay doors opened like monstrous jaws, waiting to swallow them. Matt took a steadying breath as the shuttle sailed inside and landed softly on the docking pad. The outer doors slid closed, plunging them into a gloom broken only by the red emergency lights on the floor and ceiling.

Ryce's shoulders sagged, and he wiped his forehead with his good hand. They both waited in complete silence for the lights to switch on and the shuttle's scanners to indicate the exterior pressure had been stabilized.

The communications alert beeped again, and Matt turned it on.

"Come out with your hands up," an unfamiliar voice said. "Try anything funny and you're dead."

"Can't help it, I'm a funny guy," Matt said, but the other side had already disconnected. He ran his hand over the control panel, shutting it off as Ryce deactivated his adapters.

"I guess we better get this over with," Matt said, unmoving.

Ryce rose from his chair and offered him a hand. Matt took it and stood up. His throat constricted and his palms felt clammy. At least have some dignity, he told himself. Get your act together. Don't show them you're afraid.

"Hey," Ryce said softly and tilted his chin up with a knuckle, making Matt look at him. His gray eyes were solemn. A long, charged moment passed, and then Ryce leaned in, brushing his lips against Matt's tentatively.

The kiss took him by surprise, and for a second, he stood motionless, stunned. Ryce moved to withdraw, and Matt grabbed him instinctively, deepening the kiss. It became hungry, frantic, their tongues and teeth clashing, their bodies pressed together until there was no more air in their lungs. Ryce's lips were firm and smooth, and he tasted like protein bar and crisp morning air.

"What was that for?" Matt asked after finally breaking the kiss. Ryce pulling away was like a physical loss, but Matt let his hands drop, not hindering him. It was just a kiss, he reminded himself. He'd been kissed hundreds of times. It meant nothing. Some people got hard on adrenaline; maybe Ryce did too.

"For luck." Ryce smiled faintly. There were deep shadows under his eyes, his lips slightly swollen and red against the pallid skin; Matt had never seen anyone look more beautiful.

"Whatever happens, I—" He changed what he was going to say. "—I want you to play along. Trust me."

Ryce nodded. They stepped out into the pressure chamber, and Matt threw a quick glance at the suit compartment, hoping fervently nobody would think to search it.

☆☆☆

A welcoming party was waiting for them outside. Matt took in the plasma rifles and raised his hands obediently as four men encircled them and another two hurried past into the shuttle. You had to admire the efficiency, he thought grimly as one man in the escort patted them down unhurriedly while the others kept their weapons trained on them. The guy went so far as to check Ryce's makeshift sling, making him gasp in pain. Matt had to remind himself to remain calm and quiet. Ryce's stimulant shot and painkillers were going to wear off soon, placing him in an even more vulnerable position.

The man finally finished checking them. He then wrung Matt's hands behind his back unceremoniously, snapping magnetic cuffs on his wrists. Matt wiggled his fingers experimentally, but there was no way he was getting out of them. Thankfully, they left Ryce alone for the moment, but still held them both at gunpoint.

"Come along," one of the thugs said, shoving Matt roughly and guiding him out of the underlit docking area into a narrow corridor. He resisted the urge to look back to see if the others had emerged from the shuttle.

This was no military vessel, but the ship appeared to be tightly run and well maintained. They were marched down the corridor in utter silence. Had there been only two guards, he would have seriously considered taking a shot at tackling them. Fighting dirty came easy to him when he had to. But with four of them, and with Ryce not being much help, it would amount to nothing more than a suicide attempt, and he wasn't ready for that yet.

He hoped they would be taken to the bridge, but instead, their guards ushered them into a large square cell Matt remembered only too well. This was not a good time for a panic attack, but that didn't stop his pulse from quickening and his breath from coming fast and shallow. It was the torture chamber, or what had amounted to a torture chamber when he'd been a "guest" on this ship before.

Ryce must have gathered as much from the few pairs of metal restraints hanging from the low ceiling. He balked, and one of the men shoved him hard, making him stumble and nearly sprawl on the floor. Matt didn't react, focusing instead on the man who stood in the corner, his arms crossed on his chest. He was tall, muscular to the point of being beefy, and had thick black hair and a neatly trimmed beard. The flight adapters on his temples weren't the latest issue, certainly not on the level of Ryce's implants, but then of course, Rodgers rarely piloted his own ship now. It was some feat, making the pirate wait for them instead of the other way around. The man must have been really eager to see him.

An image came unbidden to Matt—of Rodgers falling to his knees, clutching at his face and bellowing to his men, blood trickling between his fingers. By then, Matt had been in so much pain he wasn't sure if he'd actually seen that, or if his mind had pieced the scene together out of the fragments of his delirium and post-factum knowledge. It was definitely satisfying to see he'd been able to do some damage even in his most degraded state, but he was going to pay dearly for that satisfaction.

There were two other men waiting in the room with Rodgers, which made the odds even less favorable this time around.

"Spears," Rodgers said, fixing his good eye on him. Matt noted absently it was gray, the same stormy color as Ryce's eyes. Last time, he hadn't noticed that. "Long time no see. I've been looking for you."

"I'm not that hard to find," Matt said. If by some stroke of dumb luck he emerged out of this alive, he was going to strangle that little piece of shit, Pat Gentry, even if the man did surround himself with a squad of bodyguards.

Rodgers smiled. It wasn't an amused kind of smile.

"I'm here now," Matt said. "Let my ship go."

"I don't think I'm going to do that just yet," Rodgers said. "You're in no position to make demands, after all."

"Perhaps not," Matt said. Then, seizing the opportunity, he added, "But, I do have something to offer. You know, as long as you promise to release us and let my crew go unhindered."

"You think you have something to offer that would make me let your sorry ass go?" Rodgers raised an eyebrow. "This oughta be good."

It wasn't exactly boosting him with confidence, but at least Rodgers was listening, and not immediately carving him up into little pieces. So Matt continued on determinately.

"I have something valuable," he said, grasping at a half-formed idea, trying to sound as convincing as he could. "Something that's worth infinitely more than me or my entire ship."

"Matt, please think about what you're doing," Ryce said urgently. A guard standing behind him punched him in the kidneys, and Ryce doubled over, coughing. Matt ignored him.

"What do you think we were doing in this hellhole? There's a whole Mnirian complex down on one of the Colanta-3 moons. Uncharted, untapped. We were just about to go in when you hailed us."

Rodgers advanced on him, and it was all Matt could do not to recoil. The pirate stared at him, frowning. He then backhanded him across the face so hard he staggered backward.

"You think the *Mnirians* are gonna help you now? You don't get to play games with me, you little shit."

Matt licked his split lip, tasting blood.

"It's not a game," he said quickly, before Rodgers' seething anger had a chance to turn into full-blown rage. "It's true. I got a tip from a friend of mine, decided to investigate for myself. I can show you the place if you just let us go."

"Yes, you will." Rodgers grabbed his chin, fingers digging into his skin. Matt swallowed convulsively. This close, he could see glints of the electronic feed on the inner surface of the semitransparent eye patch. "There's an asteroid field around that entire planet. How'd you get past that?"

"Him." Matt tried to nod toward Ryce, but the viselike grip would allow only an infinitesimal motion. "I hired him a week ago. He's the only pilot I've ever heard of that could do it."

Out of the corner of his eye, he could see Ryce turn sharply to look at him, his face going hard, but thankfully, he kept his mouth shut. Remember what I said, Matt begged him silently. Trust me. Play along, or we're both screwed.

Rodgers' gaze shifted to Ryce, taking in his wretched state.

"No kidding. What happened to your arm?"

"A little accident with a laser blaster," Matt said hastily. Speaking while someone was squashing your face was difficult. If he could just hint how indispensable Ryce was, while creating the impression he couldn't care less for the man, perhaps the pirates would think twice about harming him. Why damage something that could prove useful, right? Unlike himself. He was of no potential use at all, but Matt tried not to think about that right now. "He still flew the shuttle all the way back. I got the location, he's got the skills to reach it, so we were gonna split the loot." Matt shrugged awkwardly. "I don't think he'll object to taking you there instead, under the circumstances."

Rodgers' fingers twisted viciously, effectively silencing him. Matt twitched, breathing noisily through his nose.

"What's your name, pretty boy?" he asked Ryce.

"Ryce Faine," he answered warily, and Matt wondered absently what his real name was. He was probably never going to find out.

"How much is this clown paying you?"

"Seven thousand creds," he said without hesitation, and Matt relaxed fractionally. At least Ryce had enough sense to back him up. Their best bet was to make Ryce appear nothing more than a random hire. Knowing what he did of Rodgers, anything more than that, and the pirate would pick the pilot apart, piece by piece, just for the pleasure of watching Matt squirm.

"Is this shit about the Mnirian place true?"

"Yes," Ryce said reluctantly.

"You seen it?"

"Yes."

"What's down there?" Rodgers asked, giving Matt a shake as if he were a kitten. He eased the pressure on Matt's jaw enough for him to give answer.

"I only know that the site is there," he said. "What's inside is anybody's guess."

"Come off it," Rodgers said. "You both willing to risk crashing and burning, you need a better incentive than 'could be anything.' I don't have patience for this shit." He shoved Matt backward. With his hands bound behind him, Matt lost his balance and fell hard, hissing in pain as he landed badly on his hip. Deciding it was safer to stay down, Matt rolled to the side, sucking on his split lip. Rodgers took a step toward him, clenching his fists.

"He's lying," Ryce said quickly, and they both turned to him. "He's knows what's there. We've been inside."

"Come on!" Matt said incredulously, sitting up awkwardly. What was Ryce thinking?!

Rodgers nodded briefly to the guard, who kicked Matt in the chest, sending him sprawling on his back again.

"I already got what I came here for, which is this piece of trash," Rodgers said, his eyes on Ryce now. "You want to cut a yourself a deal, you gotta do better than that."

Matt was too busy curling into a protective ball to watch Ryce's reaction, but his mind was racing. Rodgers was done talking to him, so all their hope rested on Ryce's shoulders. Ryce, who was a genius in almost every aspect, but a terrible liar and a shitty conspirator. The pirates wouldn't even have to torture him for information; it would be written all over his face. No, he couldn't count on him to pull him out of hot water.

"Listen," Matt began hoarsely, frantically casting about for a solution, and got kicked in the face with a boot. Red spattered the floor and his eyes swam with tears. The acute pain left him momentarily stunned, and he had to fight to maintain his grip on consciousness. He hated the taste of blood, the warm, sickening stickiness of it on his tongue and skin. And now it was pouring out of his nose, getting into his mouth, and staining the front of his shirt. If he died choking on his own blood, Tony would never let him hear the end of it.

Ryce was saying something, talking rapidly, and Matt tried to focus on the words. It was difficult; the room was spinning slowly and the floor seemed far away.

"…military bunker. I cannot guarantee we'll find anything at all, of course, but the potential value of anything Mnirian military-related could be astronomical. The problem is, of course, getting in."

"You're not the only pilot around, kid," Rodgers pointed out. Matt couldn't be sure whether he was interested. At the very least he was still listening.

"The asteroids aren't the only obstacle," Ryce said. "Even were you to land on the moon safely, you'd still have to get inside the locked structure, and I daresay you're neither equipped nor have the slightest idea as how to do that."

The cocky little bastard was going to have his teeth kicked in for talking like that, Matt thought dully. If it were Gentry they were talking to, Ryce would be rolling on the floor by now. But of course Rodgers was a different kind of psychopath, one who was more practical and liked his torture with a healthy dose of profit. If he would only listen…

"And you do?" Rodgers wasn't kicking Ryce just yet, but there was a dangerous edge to his voice.

"Yes," Ryce said. "I can fly in, and I can open the doors. That's what I was hired for in the first place. I did it for him; I can do it for you, if you agree to let me go."

"You'd sell out your boyfriend here?"

Ryce shrugged. The look he directed at Matt held nothing but mild disgust.

"He's not my boyfriend. My taste is better than that, hopefully. It was just a job. I don't know him; I don't care what you do with him. I just want to get out of this miserable place and back to civilization, and I'll need his ship to do that. He won't need it, after all. So my deal is the ship and a free pass through the jumpgate in exchange for getting you into the site."

When he'd hoped for some creative thinking on Ryce's part, Matt hadn't counted on him picking up and running with the ruse so quickly. It was hard to make sense of it. Here he was, contemplating just a few moments ago how forthright and high-minded Ryce was, how inept he was at deceit. And now, the suddenness with which the guy seemed to have picked up the basics of deception took him aback.

Rodgers looked from Matt to Ryce thoughtfully.

"Take him away," he finally said, and Matt's heart sank as a guard shoved a startled Ryce out into the corridor. His guts twisted with apprehension. The pirate followed Ryce and his escort, pausing at the door to nod at Matt's crumpled form. "Show him how much we missed him, boys."

Chapter Sixteen

The nightmare began like any other. Consciousness came slowly, the corrugated metal floor cutting into exposed skin. He blinked, trying to take stock of his body and surroundings, his thoughts sluggish, unfocused. The coppery taste in his mouth reminded him of something, but he couldn't quite recall what. Harsh overhead lights hurt his eyes; he squinted and raised a feeble hand to shield them. The room was different now, and it worried him. Where was he? Was he alone? Where was Ryce?

What a ridiculous thought. Ryce had never been in his nightmares. Ryce was probably safe in his cabin, sleeping. Matt was the only one trapped in this horror, desperately trying to wake up.

It was all wrong: the floor, the lights, the fresh blood running from his nose. None of it was as he remembered. Why couldn't he wake up?

Matt groaned and pushed himself up on one elbow. The last dregs of oblivion slipped away as cold realization sank in. Of course he couldn't wake up, because it was all real, not figments of his brain's unconscious processing. Shit, what had happened to him?

He was down in the cargo hold. That much he could gather. His captors had left the lights on and removed the magnetic cuffs for whatever reason. The room was completely bare, and he was alone. He didn't know if that was good or not.

His entire body was a tangle of aches, from his head to his ribs, and he could barely see through the narrow slit of his swollen left eye. The bruise must be spectacular. He'd been beaten within an inch of his life, and he was lucky he could move at all. But Rodgers was still not done with him; beating him into a pulp was too easy. He was just warming up for the main event.

He wiped the blood from his nose with the back of his hand and sat up. His clothes were filthy, and stank of bile. He must have vomited at one point, though thankfully he didn't remember that. It hurt to move, every muscle in his body screamed in protest as he leaned against the wall, but as far as he could tell, no limbs were broken. He was slowly thinking clearly again, though perhaps that wasn't the best thing right now.

Where was Ryce? While he was potentially more valuable to Rodgers, he was by no means safe. The guy was too pretty for his own good, especially when it came to bored pirates. His mind skittered to the press of Ryce's lips on his own, the warmth of his body, the thrumming of his heart. Remembered that.

Remembered the cold words, laced with contempt, and the ease with which he was discarded as Ryce grasped for the opportunity to save himself.

No. That felt all wrong. Matt stared at the wall, licking his torn lip, not really seeing the peeling paint. Ryce might have scorned him before, but not now, not after what they'd shared, and he was too damn good to sell Matt out to save himself. Trust me, Matt had told him. But it turned out he couldn't deliver. So Ryce had stepped up to the plate, and of course he had no way of giving Matt warning. They were running a game, a hopeless game, but if it worked, at least it would give them some time to look for a chance to escape.

It was Matt that Rodgers wanted. Matt was the one who'd underestimated Gentry's vindictiveness. Once again, he was the reason people got hurt. And this time, it was people he knew and cared about, and he hated that. This was why he'd refused to stay in the military—seeing too many people getting hurt for stupid reasons. And now he was that stupid reason. Tony, Val, and Ryce didn't deserve this. Maybe it would be better for everyone if Rodgers just killed him. The problem was his friends would still be stuck in the same mire with no one to look to for help. Not that he was much help in this situation. But at least he could try, even if it was only backing Ryce up in the desperate gambit. And he couldn't try if he was dead.

He shifted restlessly. How long had he been out? Surely, a lot could have happened while he was lying here, drooling all over the floor. Rodgers could have called Ryce on his bluff, hurt him, opened fire on his ship... He gritted his teeth in frustration. Not knowing was the hardest part, even harder than the physical pain. He almost wished for somebody to come for him, even if that meant getting beaten up again. At least he might find out what was going on.

Maybe he could even make a break for it. They wouldn't expect it of him in his state. He looked around, searching for something, anything he could use for a surprise attack when they came for him. A crate lid, a piece of loose wire. But the room apparently hadn't been utilized for quite some time, since it was completely empty and relatively clean. Perhaps it was used solely as a holding cell for unlucky hostages. Matt knew the pirates rarely kept prisoners long enough to have a proper brig.

Matt kicked the floor experimentally, aiming to dislodge one of the corrugated metal panels, but they wouldn't budge. He sat back with a sigh and ran a hand through his matted hair.

Damn it, he had to do something. He couldn't bear the thought of Ryce being out there, alone amidst a hostile crew. He was still injured; he needed medical attention, which he wasn't likely to receive here. His pain meds were bound to have worn off by now.

The door slid open, startling him out of his thoughts. He lurched to his feet, nearly falling. The man who entered was vaguely familiar. Maybe one of Rodgers' "lieutenants." He was tall and ruggedly handsome in that square-jawed kind of way. Too bad he was also holding a plasma rifle trained on Matt.

"Rested enough?" the guy said, and pointed at the door with the rifle. "Let's get going."

Two more guards, a man and a woman, were waiting in the corridor. He wasn't manhandled this time, nor were his hands bound. He wasn't sure if this was a good sign or not, but at least it gave him a semblance of dignity walking out of the cell on his own.

☆☆☆

He was fully expecting to be taken back to the torture chamber, but to his surprise the guards marched him to the bridge. He'd never actually stood on the bridge of the *Black Baza*, but of course it was no different from what he'd seen in the transmissions. It was rather small for a ship this size, a little too dark and cramped. The layout was closely modeled on that of tactical battleships, with two pilot seats and the captain's chair, with its own command panel, further behind them. Matt guessed the bow gunnery was located directly below them.

The panoramic window screen, on the other hand, was large and half-domed, allowing for excellent visibility. It showed alternating images of Colanta-3 and close-ups of the asteroid belt, both turning sluggishly in the red-tinted gloom.

Matt was surprised to see Ryce in the second pilot's seat. He definitely looked worse for wear. The tension lines around his mouth and eyes aged him, and his skin was a sickly grayish color. But his left arm was now properly bandaged, his sleeve cuffed neatly above the elbow, and there were no other signs of physical damage.

Ryce's eyes widened when he saw Matt, but he said nothing. He was probably quite a sight with his black eye and a nose so swollen it felt like it took up half his face. At least it had finally stopped bleeding.

One of the guards shoved him forward, and he struggled to keep his balance. What were they doing on the bridge? It was comforting to see Ryce relatively safe and sound, but Matt definitely wasn't ready for this turn of events. A crazy thought went through his mind—what if Rodgers had brought him here to make him watch as he blew his ship out of the sky? An eye for an eye, so to speak, and by now Rodgers would know he valued *Lisa* and her crew more than his eyesight. His pulse kicked into overdrive, and he resisted the urge to wipe his suddenly sweaty palms on his fatigues.

"Looking good there, Spears," Rodgers said, coming onto the bridge from a side door. "I'd love to see you bloodied some more, but we'll have time for that later."

"What do you want?" Matt managed to get out through the tightness in his throat.

"I want your little friend to show me all the crap you've been talking about," Rodgers said, lowering himself into the captain's chair. "See if it's really worth my time." He nodded to Ryce. "He's here. Do your thing."

Ryce turned to the pilot. Matt heard him say something to the man in a low voice.

A section of the asteroid belt came into focus, but from the ship's current position it was impossible to see the moon—it was too small and lay hidden behind the dense rocky field. However, the spherical mines were clearly visible now, and Rodgers leaned forward to take a better look. The pilot and the square-jawed lieutenant looked uneasy. Matt couldn't blame them; he remembered the sinking feeling he'd had seeing those things for the first time.

"The ship can't get past the mines, even if she could find her way around the asteroids," Ryce said, rather stating the obvious. His voice was level, but dull. He could probably do with a dose of painkillers right now. Matt's head was throbbing as though someone were hammering nails into his temples. "The only way down is with a shuttle or a fighter jet."

"What are the coordinates of the site?" Rodgers asked.

Ryce shook his head. God knew he could be stubborn, but the problem was, the pirates were much less likely to put up with it than Matt. As if to illustrate this point, the guard standing next to Ryce hit him across the face. It was a casual blow, without any real heat behind it, a warning. It still made Ryce's head snap back, and Matt looked away, trying his best not to flinch.

Ryce glared at the guard as he briefly touched his reddened cheek, but turned to Rodgers when he spoke.

"I don't have the coordinates," he said. "They were logged into the shuttle computer, but Mr. Spears wiped it clean when you hailed us."

"You were there," Rodgers pointed out.

"Yes, but I don't remember them off the top of my head," Ryce said. Matt had to give him credit for not stumbling over what amounted to the biggest falsehood in the universe. The man was rapidly adapting to the whole lying through his teeth thing. "Spears knows them, though." He nodded to Matt.

"Ugh," Matt said, momentarily blindsided. Rodgers fixed his one-eyed gaze on him, as if considering the best tactic for extracting information. Was Ryce *trying* to have him tortured? How was he supposed to play that up? "I, ugh…"

"He can come with us," Ryce said quickly, cutting off whatever response Matt was about to offer. "It will be faster. I'm assuming you can make him give up the coordinates eventually, but I would rather not linger here more than necessary."

"You might be underestimating my methods," Rodgers said, still watching Matt. "But I do want to take my time with him. Are you gonna cooperate, Spears?"

"Yes," Matt said dryly. He didn't know what exactly Ryce was planning, but he was more than happy to seize the opportunity. Being on a shuttle with a few armed pirates was better than being on a ship with a lot of armed pirates, after all. And he was going to take any chance he could to stay his execution. "As long as you release my ship."

Rodgers' expression told him everything he needed to know about his negotiation skills. But it was damn hard to be suave with a black eye and a plasma rifle pointed at his back.

Rodgers nodded at the man standing behind Matt. "Take him out of here, Pearce." Square-jaw stepped up and grabbed his arm, hauling Matt off the bridge and into the corridor, where the other guards waited. Matt wanted to tell them he could do very well with verbal instructions. But he knew better than to bet on their sense of humor, so he shut up and followed them in silence back to his holding cell.

☆☆☆

It was a good thing they'd had a chance to grab something to eat back on the shuttle, because nobody seemed concerned with feeding him. Only after Rodgers had made it clear Matt was to be kept alive for a little while longer was he given a bottle of water and a turn at using a bathroom. He made the most of it, glad of the chance to freshen up and take a piss. The stench of sweat and vomit clinging to his clothes was almost as bad as the headache and swelling around his nose and bruised eye.

To his surprise, he was taken to his own shuttle rather than one of the *Baza*'s landing vessels. He had to make a conscious effort not to glance at the space suits lined up in the see-through hallway compartments for assurance they hadn't been tampered with. Though, if the pirates had found the warhead, he probably wouldn't be sitting here right now, whether they'd figured out what the thing was or not.

Pearce, who accompanied him the entire time, shoved him into one of the passenger seats, none too gently. He was clearly not on board with the idea of an impromptu scavenging expedition, though of course he hadn't said anything in Matt's hearing.

The cramped interior was not conducive to using cumbersome rifles, so Pearce opted for a short-range handgun, which was entirely unnecessary, in Matt's opinion, given that his hands were firmly bound behind his back again. The man sat in the adjacent chair, giving him a look of controlled animosity.

"If you even think of trying something funny," he said, "I'm going to pick up whatever is left of you after the captain is done, and make you beg to be thrown in the airlock."

Apparently, no amount of chiseled jaw could prevent one from being a total asshole.

"Fuck you too," Matt muttered. Pearce's eyes narrowed, but Matt was saved by the arrival of Rodgers and Ryce.

Ryce looked marginally better. But Matt could tell the injury was bothering him as he lowered himself gingerly into the pilot seat. Rodgers motioned for Pearce to come with him. They both left the shuttle, talking in low voices, but not before Pearce threw him a warning look. Matt mentally flipped him off and then turned to Ryce quickly, taking advantage of the intermission.

"Are you all right?" he asked, lowering his voice to a whisper.

"As well as can be expected," Ryce said. His gaze swept over Matt, filling with concern. "You aren't, though."

"I'm fine," Matt said. He really was, considering the alternative. "What are you doing?"

"Right now, stalling for time. Remember the coordinates," Ryce said, and fired off a series of figures that Matt struggled to retain. It did nothing for his headache. "I know what I'm doing; just bear with me on this one." He didn't sound or looked too sure, but Matt nodded anyway. They had no other choice. He hoped Tony could think of some way to get through the jumpgate or get out of the pirate ship's range without drawing too much heat in the time they'd bought, because God knew he was out of ideas at this point.

"How come we're using our shuttle?" he asked.

"I insisted I needed it to go back to the *Lisa* once they've seen the site." Ryce shrugged. "Rodgers wasn't too happy about that, but it's smaller than their shuttlecraft. Faster, too. Val really did a fine job on it."

"I'm sure it'll be a comforting thought in his last moments," Matt said.

Ryce smiled wryly and was about to say something else when the pirates' footsteps echoed in the hallway. He clamped down, turning back to the control panel.

Matt focused his attention on the stain patterns that adorned his pants, avoiding looking at either of the men, not wanting to appear defiant. This time, Rodgers and Pearce were accompanied by a third man, who was also carrying a gun.

Pearce sat down next to Matt, glaring at him like the entire thing was his fault, while Rodgers took the copilot seat. He nodded to Ryce, who then touched his adapters. The control panel lit up, and the engines purred like a giant cat waking up from slumber. The third guy sat behind Matt.

"All right," Rodgers said, getting comfortable as if he were sitting in his own captain's chair on the bridge of the *Baza*. "Take us for a ride."

Chapter Seventeen

The shuttle was originally designed for six passengers, but with five people, it already felt crowded, even without taking the guns into account. Matt was acutely aware of Pearce sitting next to him, his body rigid with tension. Pearce had made it clear he suspected a trap or some sort of foul play on Matt and Ryce's side. Matt didn't bother telling him he was giving them a lot more credit than they deserved.

Stalling for time was really their best tactic right now, but Ryce must have had some kind of endgame in mind. At least, that was what Matt was hoping for, since it was abundantly clear to everybody involved Rodgers wasn't going to let any of them go.

He cast about discreetly, looking for anything they could use to their advantage, considering the possibilities. Ryce was the one connected to the shuttle computer, and Rodgers was watching him like a hawk. He wouldn't have many opportunities for subterfuge, and with all of them confined to the same space, Matt couldn't think of a way to incapacitate the pirates specifically. Unless Ryce was planning on tackling them somehow on the ground, which, considering the sorry condition they were both in, appeared equally unlikely. Then again, if they were to go inside the abandoned base again, they had the advantage of prior acquaintance. Perhaps Ryce was planning to trap the pirates inside somehow, much like they were trapped themselves, and seize the opportunity to get away. Or perhaps he had no plan at all and was winging it as he went along. Matt wished they had some way of communicating to each other that was more reliable than glances and guesswork, but of course that was impossible.

Anyway, Ryce had other concerns at the moment, having to concentrate on navigating the spacecraft through the minefield yet again. Doing it with an injured arm, and the added threat of a gun pointed at his head, was tremendously risky even with whatever painkillers and stimulants he'd been given by the medics on the *Baza*. Maybe it would be better if they crashed into a rock, Matt thought bitterly. God, he needed a drink so bad. Maybe he could ask for a bottle of whiskey as his last dying wish.

The shuttle shook a few times as smaller debris along the edge of the field skidded across the hull. Matt thought absently about how battered it must be by now, and how pissed Val would be at having to fix all of it, if he ever saw the shuttle again.

Ryce was intent on the screen, his fingers white on the control stick. Matt didn't know how long he had been out in his holding cell, but it couldn't have been long. Between getting his wound tended and answering Rodgers' questions, Ryce probably hadn't had a chance to get any sleep, and they'd already been running on fumes. Matt had never liked using stimulants on principle, especially not consecutively, like Ryce must have been doing now. Stims made you agitated, and that wasn't a desired condition in a pilot on a precarious mission. And while Matt was fully prepared to go down if it meant taking Rodgers with him, he didn't want Ryce to die for something that was entirely not his doing. Matt had to make it through.

"The coordinates," Rodgers said without looking at him. Pearce gave Matt a stern look, but there was no need for intimidation. He repeated the string of numbers, praying he'd remembered all of them correctly, and watched as the flight computer zoomed in on the location.

Just as before, Ryce ignored the suggested route and picked his own course.

Matt half-expected Pearce to turn and shoot him in the chest now that he had nothing more to offer in terms of usefulness, but of course Rodgers wanted to have some alone time with him later. Ryce, on the other hand, stood a good chance of getting shot the minute their shuttle touched the floor of the *Baza*'s docking bay. If he was lucky.

The journey was taking longer this time. Of course, the trajectory was longer, and there was always the revolving belt to factor in, but they were also going more slowly. Ryce was taking his time, dodging every big chunk of rock and the occasional mine with the same precision but much less fluidly. It was a relief when the moon finally came into full view before them.

Its gray gashed surface appeared as lifeless and raw as before. It was difficult to grasp that so much potential death and destruction lay hidden under the colorless façade. Perhaps there was more down there than they'd had the chance to see; and the thought of taking the pirates there, with the ultimate doomsday weapon stashed within easy reach, made Matt supremely uncomfortable. But there was nothing, absolutely nothing he could do about it at this point.

"Do you know where to land?" Rodgers asked.

"I think so," Ryce said, without batting an eye. There was no doubt in Matt's mind he remembered every single piece of data that led him to the right location in the first place.

The shuttle tilted, barely avoiding being crushed between two huge asteroids, and began its descent. The occurrence of "field mines" was noticeably higher in the immediate proximity of the moon, and Matt decided he wasn't going to watch Ryce dodging them.

Instead he focused on his recollection of the layout of the Mnirian base, trying to come up with a scenario that would allow them to use the alien structure to their advantage. The fact that Ryce was the only one who knew how to work the door-controlling mechanisms tipped the odds slightly in their favor, but he couldn't imagine either Rodgers or Pearce giving them the opportunity to handle the lasers unattended. Maybe if they could somehow trap the pirates in the lower corridors using the elevator mechanism? Even if the pirates managed to emerge from the tunnels, much like they had, both he and Ryce would be long gone by then. That would leave the *Black Baza* and its crew to contend with, of course, but they could figure that out once safely back on the *Lisa*.

There was the small jolt of the bottom thrusters kicking in as the shuttle glided above the moon's surface. The landing was considerably less graceful than could be expected. By the time the spacecraft came to a complete rest, Ryce's hands were shaking so badly Matt was half-expecting Rodgers to forcibly take control. They touched down on nearly the same spot as before, though, so Matt had a pretty good grip on the direction, in case they had to utilize an impromptu escape route.

Next to him, Pearce let out a sigh of relief. It probably wasn't even conscious, but Matt could wholeheartedly agree. He didn't know how long the flight had lasted, probably no longer than an hour and a half, but it was one of the longest and least pleasant hours of his life, the hours of him being beaten within an inch of his life excluded, of course. But they were here, in one piece, and all the balls were still up in the air.

"Get on with it," Pearce said, nudging him roughly.

"I can't get on with cuffs, can I?" Matt retorted. "Unless you wanna just leave me here to chill while you go on your little day trip. I'm cool with that."

"Shut up," Pearce warned, but unlocked his cuffs so Matt could put on a space suit.

All his aches and pains came rushing back as he got out of the chair. He heard Rodgers contacting the ship with their exact position and ordering it to stand by, awaiting further notification within three hours. That didn't give them much time, considering they were pretty much flying by the seat of their pants. The third man, Claes, was to remain on the shuttle to serve as a point of contact in case anything went wrong. Matt had to keep moving, and his first step was toward the suit that held the Mnirian warhead in its kit. He definitely didn't want either of the pirates discovering it by mistake when they suited up.

Matt took off his sweat- and blood-stained fatigues and donned the space suit under Pearce's watchful eye. As he struggled with the fastenings with swollen fingers, Ryce stepped into the narrow corridor, followed by Rodgers. He looked like death on legs again. Matt hoped he'd brought another dose of stimulants with him; otherwise, there was no chance he could make the journey back, assuming they would be making it alive.

Ryce put on his own suit without saying a word, wincing when he had to take off the sling to put his arm into the sleeve. Both pirates geared up one at a time, taking the time to inspect their suits; they seemed familiar with how they operated.

"I need the laser," Ryce said once everybody was ready, and the suits' sensors indicated they were fully charged and operational.

Matt opened the kit and handed him the laser generator, taking this opportunity to make sure the warhead was still there as well, safely tucked at the bottom of the bag. He was lucky his bet paid off, and the pirates weren't thorough when searching the unused space suit compartments.

"What's that?" Pearce asked, grabbing the device before Ryce could touch it.

"That's our key for getting inside," Ryce said irritably.

"It's a high-powered laser," Pearce said, turning it in his hands.

"It's a Mnirian site, for fuck's sake," Matt interjected before Ryce could say something that could set the pirate off. Matt set them off simply by breathing; so one more smart-ass remark wouldn't make a difference. "Of course we'd need a laser. What did you think we used to open the door, a crowbar?"

His suit being up was all that saved him from being hit in the face again, as Pearce's glare clearly indicated.

"Give me that," Rodgers said, taking the device and putting it in his hip pack. "Now get moving."

☆☆☆

Before they could step out into the airlock, however, the screen lit up, flashing notification of an incoming transmission.

"Captain," Claes called. "I think you'll want to see this."

Rodgers pushed Ryce out of his way and took the pilot seat, removing his helmet and tapping his adapters to establish a link.

A live feed of the *Black Baza* bridge appeared on-screen.

"Captain," Rodgers' first officer said, "there's an incoming vessel at the jumpgate."

Pearce tightened his hand on his gun. This was like a bad *déjà vu*; the pirates obviously hadn't been expecting any trouble in this distant region of the galaxy.

"What kind of vessel?" Rodgers asked.

The officer glanced sideways to read the incoming data.

"Federation Fleet. D-class battle cruiser."

The tension, which was already running high aboard the shuttle, skyrocketed. Matt caught Ryce's indrawn breath and his stare, but he couldn't decipher his expression. If by some stroke of luck it was the Fleet hunting down the pirates, Matt didn't want to be caught in the crossfire, and he definitely didn't want to explain what they were doing here if they were captured. But if it came to taking his chances on being in trouble with the Federation versus being in trouble with Rodgers, he'd choose the Federation any day. Whether he'd get the chance to actually make the choice remained to be seen. A D-class cruiser was a midsized battleship, fast and heavily armed, but it didn't carry combat fighter craft, so it was a pretty evenly matched with a heavy raider like the *Black Baza*.

"On-screen," Rodgers said.

"Transmitting," the first officer said, and the image changed to display the other ship, silhouetted against the reddish glow reflected off the rims of the jumpgate. It was unmistakably a Fleet cruiser; a six-digit number and the name *Achilles* were emblazoned in stark white across its flank. The name was vaguely familiar, but there was no way Matt could remember every ship in the Fleet.

"It's hailing us, Captain." The officer's voice came over the image.

"Transfer the signal here; voice only. You two, stay back and be quiet," he said over his shoulder to Ryce and Matt.

The feeling of *déjà vu* intensified. Matt discreetly touched the bag on his suit to reassure himself the warhead was nestled safely inside. Whatever happened now, he couldn't let the thing fall into the wrong hands.

"Commodore Archer of the UFF *Achilles*," a deep male voice said over the transmission link. "Identify yourself."

Matt's stomach twisted, and he shot a quick glance at Ryce. So the mysterious Mr. Ari had finally shown himself. But why now, in this exact moment? He was taking a huge risk in coming here so openly; unless he knew somehow of the predicament they were in and had decided to take care of the problem.

"You know who this is," Rodgers replied, unfazed. "What do you want?"

"I'm given to understand that you are holding a Federation Fleet officer prisoner aboard your ship," Archer said dryly. Ryce cringed.

"Ain't any I'm aware of," Rodgers said.

"I'm not here to play games," Archer said. "Put him on."

Rodgers turned around and motioned for Ryce to take off his helmet and take the seat next to him.

"I'm assuming he's talking about you," he said. "Ain't no way that gutter rat"—he gestured to Matt—"suddenly became a Fleet officer. Connecting video feed."

Matt snorted hysterically. Pearce jammed the butt of the gun into his side to quiet him, and the snort turned into a grunt. He had to give it to Rodgers for keeping it cool under pressure, though. Most men, even hardened criminals, would panic when faced with the threat of a Federation cruiser.

The image on-screen changed to show a darkened room rather than a bridge. Commodore Archer, a solid gray-haired man in his fifties, clad in a severe dark-gray Fleet uniform, was sitting behind a desk. A large interactive star map was displayed in the background.

"Nice to see you in good health, Mr. Faine," he said, putting a slight emphasis on the name.

"Commodore," Ryce said, sounding sheepish.

Archer turned his attention to Rodgers.

"I'm ordering you to surrender the captives and release their spacecraft," he said. "Otherwise I will be forced to take over your ship."

"Let me think about it," Rodgers said and cut communication. The screen went abruptly black, and the sudden silence settled like a tangible thing, taking up all the space inside the shuttle. Pearce and Claes looked uneasy, but to their credit, they said nothing to contradict Rodgers in front of the prisoners.

"Fleet officer," Rodgers said, biting out the words.

The hairs rose on the back of Matt's neck. Shit, this was bad. Archer was betting on intimidating Rodgers by pulling rank, but Rodgers wasn't one to take well to ultimatums. Archer, even backed by his very own battleship, was a long way away, and Ryce was right here. The thought must have dawned on Ryce as well, because he turned another shade of pale and visibly shrank in his seat.

"Did you know about this?" Rodgers asked, turning to Matt.

He shook his head. "Faine must have gone rogue," he said, thinking quickly. "I just hired him last week, like I told you. I didn't know he was a fugitive. They must be wanting to put him on trial for defection or something."

"Bullshit," Rodgers said. "Ain't no one sending a whole cruiser off its course for one deserter. Unless he knows something important." He turned back to Ryce. "What is it?"

"There is nothing," Ryce said. "He's right. I ran. I only took this job to get as far away as I could. I had no idea they'd chase me all the way out here."

Rodgers grabbed Ryce by his left shoulder and shook him, making him cry out in pain. With his other hand, he pulled a long steel knife from inside his boot and brought it close to Ryce's face. The younger man recoiled, but Rodgers held him fast.

"You can ask your friend here how it feels when your adapters are cut right out of your head," Rodgers said, looking Ryce straight in the eyes. "I was kinda surprised he survived that. Want to see if you'll be as lucky?"

Bile rose in Matt's throat at the sight of utter terror in Ryce's eyes. He shied away from the memory of it as if from a blade, as though mere recollection could hurt him. The pain had been excruciating, almost too much to take in, and he was grateful he could no longer remember all the details. Rodgers was right; he'd been lucky. The adapters were fused directly to nerve endings in the brain; tearing them out so brutally could have easily left him a cripple or a blubbering idiot. If he didn't die on the spot, that is. He couldn't take that chance with Ryce.

"Wait," he said, his voice sounding foreign to his own ears. "Let him go. I'll tell you everything you want to know."

Chapter Eighteen

"Then spill," Rodgers said, not moving the knife.

"Matt, don't," Ryce said in a low voice. Perhaps he was right, but Matt knew all too well that the pirate would have no qualms about carrying out his threats, the presence of a Federation vessel notwithstanding.

"I'm working for that guy," Matt motioned to the screen that had held Archer's image a moment ago. "We both are, actually—Faine as a pilot, me as a scavenger. Faine told you we didn't know what was down there; that's a lie. The Commodore knew exactly what he was looking for."

"What is it?" Rodgers asked.

"Matt," Ryce said warningly.

"Shut up," Matt told him fiercely. Don't you see I'm trying to take his attention off you, he screamed in his head. Shut the fuck up before he guts you like a fish. "You had your chance. If you want to get your brain torn to pieces, go ahead, but I'm not going to risk that for the sake of your commander."

He turned to Rodgers. "It's some sort of a weapon. He didn't trust us enough to specify, but it's something big. We were supposed to find and deliver it without alerting anybody."

"Good job," Pearce said mockingly.

"And I bet Central Command doesn't know about his little side operation," Rodgers said. He withdrew the knife from Ryce's temple, but didn't put it away. "What else?"

"That's it," Matt shrugged. He was taking a huge risk telling Rodgers all that, but he had the advantage of having the warhead stowed safely in his bag. At least, that's what he was telling himself. If the pirates hadn't already searched their kits, there was no reason for them to do so now, especially when he was directing the focus toward the base itself. "He was telling the truth about that part. I mean, getting into the site. We were searching for it when the call came through about your ship."

"The honorable commander there might be willing to shell out some cash for that thing," Rodgers said to Pearce. "Not to mention giving us the all clear. Think he'll give a damn about his precious officer then?"

"You still want to go down there?" Pearce asked. He looked even less thrilled about the prospect than before. It was the first time Matt had seen him openly question his captain's decisions.

"Damn right. If we find this shit, it'll give us enough leverage with the commodore." To Claes, he said, "Alert the *Baza*; this might take longer than we think. Let them contact the *Achilles* for more time." He got up and slipped the knife in his boot. "You two, gear up. And if I find out you've been keeping other stuff from me, you're gonna wish I'd cut you now."

Ryce all but leapt out of the chair and pushed past Matt into the corridor, even as Claes took up his place at the controls. Matt wished he could say something, to make Ryce at least look him in the eye, but he couldn't, and damn it, he was winging it for both their sakes. So what if, despite Matt's best intentions, Ryce's worries about alerting the pirates to the existence of a superweapon ultimately came true. He was buying them time, and every minute they were still alive and whole counted. Let this Archer guy wrack his brains as to how he was going to rescue them and get his little present. He was the one with Fleet resources at his disposal, for fuck's sake.

"I said, gear up!" Rodgers barked, and Matt rushed to check the fastenings and the inner data feed. Ryce put his helmet on and did the same, still avoiding eye contact, and a few moments later they were joined by the two pirates.

"All right then," Rodgers said, once everybody was ready. "Let's go."

Ryce stepped out into the airlock, followed by Matt, with Rodgers and Pearce bringing up the rear.

The harsh lights from the shuttle illuminated their way across what was becoming familiar terrain. Both Rodgers and Pearce had their guns out and were scanning the surroundings as if they expected a squad of Federation troopers to spring up in an ambush. Matt noted that Rodgers' weapon was set on low impact, meant to incapacitate rather than kill. Pearce's wasn't.

The cave mouth, despite the utter darkness within, looked less ominous this time, perhaps because their escort presented a more pressing threat. The loose gravel slipped beneath their graviboots as they entered the opening, moving out of range of the shuttle projectors, and the sound of their breathing in the earpieces was now multiplied by two. The silvery streaks in the walls shone as they caught the light from their guns and helmets, but they didn't stop to look at the unique patterns.

The closed double doors at the end of the cave gave Matt pause. He was fully expecting to find them open, just as they'd been left, but they must have automatically shut when the security system had gone off down in the warhead chamber. For all he knew, it was still on, shooting needle-sharp laser beams across the room.

He hadn't thought about it before, but now he couldn't get it out of his mind, even as Rodgers fiddled with the laser generator under Ryce's instructions. Could the security system have triggered other mechanisms and traps besides simply closing the doors? He had no idea what they were going to encounter on the upper levels. Would it even be possible for them to enter the tunnels again? If not, perhaps it was for the best, but on the other hand, if the security system was still activated, they could use that to their advantage. But that room was a long way down, and whether they could actually make it there was still up in the air.

☆☆☆

The white glimmer of the metal door corners drew Matt's attention, and he watched as the doors opened again. As far as he could see, there was nothing inside that would indicate trouble, no movement or flashing lights, just the silent darkness.

"Well, shit," Pearce said succinctly, staring into the stillness. Matt couldn't help but notice he seemed hesitant about stepping inside.

Rodgers motioned for Ryce to go in first and followed him, holding the gun in one hand and the laser in the other.

"I'm assuming these are yours," he remarked, indicating the two sets of fresh boot prints on the dusty floor ahead of them. He looked around, his flashlight sliding off the slick walls and columns. Oily black shadows slithered away from the light and coalesced in its wake.

Matt was no less hesitant about proceeding, even though his fears regarding the possible effects of the downstairs alarm seemed unfounded. They followed the path of their boot prints as Ryce led their little party to the circular engraving in the center of the floor. Unsurprisingly, the pattern looked intact, as if it had never moved. The only indication of any disturbance was the poorly swept dust around it. Matt shivered slightly as he remembered last seeing the platform, back in its place, its solid stone column rising above them and sealing their only way out.

Rodgers held Ryce at gunpoint, point-blank, as he handed him the generator to be adjusted to the new pattern. Matt kept quiet. He could tell the unfamiliar setting was making Pearce nervous, and he didn't want to get shot because someone got too fidgety.

"Stand back," Ryce warned, and Matt and Pearce took a wary step back from the etched circle, while he and Rodgers remained standing in the middle of it, holding the device above the tiny keyhole. The laser beams shot out just as they had before, forming the impressive beam that would trigger the keyhole. The thin lines shone brightly and the platform began to descend. They all stepped hurriedly onto it, huddling together. Ryce handed the generator back to Rodgers without being prompted.

The platform slid smoothly down until coming to the floor level with the two opposing tunnels. Truth be told, Matt couldn't remember which one was which—which tunnel led to the chamber where they had found the warhead and triggered the security system, and which tunnel led to the empty chamber where they had made their daring escape. He peered into the darkness, trying to determine the correct alignment with relation to the rectangular hall above them, but he hadn't been paying attention to the directions in the first place.

"Where does this lead?" Rodgers asked, looking every which way.

Matt fumbled for a second. They couldn't even pretend they hadn't reached this level, since their footprints gave them away.

"There are other rooms at each end," he said finally, stalling as he tried to decide how much information to give out. "We didn't have the chance to explore all of them. But there's some interesting kind of machinery in one of them we didn't get a chance to look at closely."

"It's that way," Ryce said, suddenly coming to his aid and pointing to the northeast tunnel. Matt threw him a quick look. Was that the correct direction? Of course both chambers were empty; there was nothing for the pirates to find there anymore. But at the very least, they might win some time for Archer to get his act together.

Rodgers hesitated for a moment. If he suspected some sort of trick and decided to take the opposite direction... Matt frantically raked his brain for some way to convince him without sounding even more suspicious, but thankfully the pirate seemed to take Ryce at his word and gestured for him to take the lead with his gun.

They started down the corridor, with the pirates taking the rear, their guns at the ready. Matt's battered body protested against the exertion, even as mild as walking along a corridor, and he dragged his feet, earning himself a few shoves from Pearce. Even breathing was difficult, pain radiating in his chest with each intake of oxygen. The men who had beat him up must have cracked a rib or two, but at least nothing was broken as far as he could tell. His mind was racing now, trying to come up with a possible plan. Would the laser defense still be on in there? Maybe it had shut down after a while, just like all the doors closing at some point after they'd left.

The tension was becoming unbearable, especially with the thing in Matt's kit that seemed to weigh more than all the rock above their heads. The tunnel seemed to stretch forever. Was it the same one? Surely, they'd been walking for too long.

"Here it is," Ryce said, suddenly coming to a halt. Matt peered into the entrance past his shoulder. The helmet lights picked up the huge cannon in the middle of the chamber.

"What is that?" Pearce asked from behind them.

Ryce moved inside without answering. The four of them circled the rotund plinth, their lights flooding the chamber as they examined the machinery and the glowing etchings around the base. This was definitely the first cannon chamber; there were no traces of laser cuts on the wall or the cannon having been activated, and the roof was in place. His heart beat faster with cautious hope. If only the laser light show was still on in the back room...

"This thing looks like a plasma cannon," Pearce said, stepping closer to examine the control panel mechanism. Apparently he was smarter than Matt, or more familiar with various weapons systems, for figuring that out so quickly. He poked the black blocks experimentally, and snatched his hand back when they moved gently under his touch, the symbols upon them glowing blue.

"This is the weapon your boss wanted?" Rodgers asked. He didn't join his lieutenant, but kept a watchful eye on his prisoners instead. "A little big for the two of you to haul out of here."

"I don't know," Ryce said. "Like we said, we had no time to look around beyond this point."

"What's there?" Pearce asked. He'd left the cannon and wandered around the room, coming to stand in front of the narrow door at the back.

Matt's heartbeat quickened. This was his chance; he might not get another. He edged closer, moving to where Pearce was standing and keeping to the shadowy recesses behind one of the pillars. His mouth was dry, with an unpleasant, sour aftertaste, as if he'd just woken up with an epic hangover without the perks of having actually drunk himself into a stupor.

Rodgers joined Pearce by the door.

"Open it," he told Ryce, who took the laser generator and slowly adjusted the settings. Matt's heart was beating so fast he was sure everybody could hear it over the link. Pearce and Rodgers' attention seemed to be fixed on the doorway at the moment, and he tensed, waiting for the right moment, that window of opportunity.

Ryce took a step back as the beams shot out to touch the four corners of the door. He glanced quickly at Matt as he did so, mouthing the word "now."

The door slid into the wall, and they were instantly overwhelmed with the blinding light coming from the inside. It seemed that despite Matt's worries, the security system hadn't shut off on its own. There was a split second of confusion, and he seized it, lunging at Pearce, who was standing closest to him, and shoving him into the room crisscrossed with moving laser beams. The pirate stumbled forward with a curse that turned into a scream as one of the beams caught him sideways in the chest. He crumpled in a heap on the floor, just within the chamber, as his gun fell from his hand. His suit's sensors went crazy, beeping insistently over their commlink.

Matt quickly activated the reflective visor to shield his eyes from the blue glare. He saw Ryce tackle Rodgers, but he was too slow and too weak. And the sudden onslaught of the lasers and Pearce's screams were enough of a warning that Rodgers was able to twist and counter Ryce's pounce with a vicious hit to his injured arm with the butt of his gun. Ryce cried out and hunched over, at the same time dropping the laser generator he'd been holding. Rodgers kicked him hard, knocking him down, and then stomped on his chest with his graviboot. Matt flinched, suddenly feeling the ache in his own ribs in reaction as he watched the savage attack. Ryce jerked and then lay still, sprawled on his back like a broken doll.

"No!" Matt made a move in his direction, but stopped in his tracks when Rodgers turned, pointing the gun at him. He tapped on the side of his helmet twice, turning on the visor just as Matt had done.

"I'm gonna kill you, bitch," he snarled.

Matt shut his eyes against the blast that was about to tear into his chest. He'd heard that people's lives flashed before their eyes in moments like these, but his mind was absolutely blank, paralyzed. He couldn't pray or hope or beg; all he could manage was not staring down the barrel of the gun as it went off.

"Captain, we have an incoming." Claes's voice suddenly came over the link. The transmission sounded distorted. Something in the layers of solid rock around them must have been interfering with the signal.

"What is it?"

Matt risked opening his eyes. Rodgers was still holding him at gunpoint, still looking pissed off. Matt wisely kept his mouth shut and didn't move.

"Another Federation vessel, sir. A destroyer battleship."

"You've got to be kidding me," Rodgers said. "This place is like the fucking Sawyer Strait."

Out of the corner of his eye, Matt saw Ryce stirring from his prostrate position. His heart leaped, but he kept his gaze on Rodgers, not wanting to give Ryce away. Of course, if Rodgers wanted to kill Ryce, he would have done it. Matt wondered why he hadn't. Then it occurred to him that the pirate still needed Ryce. How else would he get back to the upper levels on his own?

"They're ordering the *Black Baza* to stand down and surrender. Brock's asking for your orders, sir."

Matt made himself focus on Rodgers' eye patch. Behind the pirate's back, Ryce slowly pushed himself up, leaning on his good elbow, his left arm at an awkward angle. He crawled toward Pearce's discarded weapon, which thankfully had landed on this side of the threshold. With luck, Rodgers would be too preoccupied to notice, but the moment he turned his head he would see him reaching for the gun.

"Order him to contact the *Achilles* and tell Commodore Archer to get that destroyer off my ass if he wants his pilot back," Rodgers said.

"He can't," Matt put in, before his sense of self-preservation could stop him from deflecting Rodgers' attention from what was going on behind him. "What—do you think they're really here for you? You're just a bonus. They're here to nab one of their own that's gone rogue. We're probably way down on his priorities list right now."

Of course that was pure guesswork on his part. He had no idea what that destroyer was doing here, but right now he couldn't care less if it was the admiral's own private yacht. His only concern was stalling long enough for Ryce to rally. He was nearly there, but his injuries were clearly slowing him down.

"Shut up," Rodgers told him. "The only reason you're still alive is because shooting you is too easy. Flap your gums again and I'll blast your fucking head off."

Matt raised his hands in acquiescence. Ryce's fingers closed on the gun, and he rolled onto his back. The motion must have registered in Rodgers' peripheral vision. As he whirled around, Matt hurled himself at him before he could aim the gun at Ryce, and they both stumbled into the cannon plinth. Ryce scooted over, nearly dropping the gun as he tried to raise it.

"Matt, get down!" he shouted.

Matt grunted in response. He was grappling with Rodgers, desperately hanging on for dear life to his gun arm as the other man flung him against the moving blocks of the control panel. The jolt sent a surge of pain through Matt's battered body that nearly made him lose his grip. But he couldn't let go. He knew the second he did, the pirate would kill them both. It also meant he couldn't duck to allow Ryce a clear shot.

"Captain?" Claes asked worriedly over the link, alarmed by the verbal struggle. "Sir, what's going on?"

Rodgers ignored him. He grabbed Matt's wrist and twisted it viciously, making him loosen his grip, while simultaneously flinging him forward. Matt stumbled, but Rodgers' hold prevented him from falling on his face. The pirate reeled him in, sticking the gun under his ribs. Ryce froze, crouched on the floor, Pearce's plasma gun pointed in their direction. For a split second, they were all poised in a mute tableau.

"You, Fleet officer," Rodgers said. "Push that thing over here. Careful, now."

Ryce lowered the gun slowly and slid it across the floor toward Rodgers. The pirate shoved it farther aside with his foot, out of their reach, and pushed Matt hard, knocking him onto the floor.

"I'm getting really tired of your shit," Rodgers said. "Time's up, Spears." He raised his gun and shot Matt square in the chest.

Chapter Nineteen

It was like being hit by a freight barge. The impact of the blast knocked the wind out of him, plastering him to the floor. Everything around him receded as he gasped frantically for air; even the ensuing beeping of his suit's alarm seemed distant. All Matt could do was watch in a daze as Rodgers stooped to pick up Pearce's gun and holstered it.

"Captain!" Claes's voice came over the link, muffled as if from a great distance yet clear in its urgency. "Captain, they're getting ready to open fire."

"Tell them to hold their shit together. I'm coming." Rodgers walked around Matt's prostrate form, without so much as casting a second glance either at him or Pearce's body, and picked up the laser generator from where Ryce had dropped it.

"On your feet, Faine. We're leaving," he said, turning to Ryce.

Matt, still struggling to regain his breath, turned his head cautiously toward them. Their voices came as if from under water, booming and distorted. He tried to draw a deeper breath, and the pain hit him. His heart beat against his fractured ribs like a caged animal, threatening to break through the weakened bars. The sturdy suit had absorbed most of the energy of the blast without disintegrating on the spot. But at such close range, the damage must have been extensive, even with Rodgers' gun being set on low impact. As far as he could tell, all the systems were shutting down, and he didn't need the computer to tell him that with the suit inactivated, he was going to run out of oxygen very soon.

"No," Ryce said stubbornly. He crouched on the floor, the reflective surface of his helmet now hiding his expression.

"I don't have time for this," Rodgers said, pointing the gun at Ryce's head. "Either you get up now, or never. Your choice."

"Ryce, don't," Matt said, though all he managed was a whisper, and he wasn't sure the others picked up on it. He lifted his hand with an effort that took much of his remaining strength, and waved him away feebly. "Just go with him."

There was nothing Ryce could do here anyway. Matt was going to die very shortly, but at least Ryce had some sort of a chance. Perhaps either Archer or the other Fleet commanders would find a way to extricate him. Dying together might seem like the romantic thing to do, but Matt had never held on to any such notions.

Ryce turned to him sharply, his face nothing more than a pale smear behind the shiny coated glass. He pushed himself up to his feet with visible effort, hampered by whatever injuries Rodgers' kick might have inflicted, but still hesitated.

"Matt..."

"Move it!" Rodgers shoved him roughly toward the mouth of the tunnel. "Your buddy can wait here till we get this crap sorted. Can't drag his ass all the way up now. If he croaks, serves him right for killing my man. Too bad I got no time to watch."

In a few steps, they were both swallowed by the ever-present darkness, and Matt was left alone. The only sound now was the sobbing of his breath. The suit's beeping alarm had died out, and even the helmet light was growing dimmer.

He was shaking. With nerves or cold, he couldn't tell, but the climate control was slowly failing like the rest of the systems, and the ambient temperature here was lower than on the moon's surface. It was a close race between freezing and suffocating when the suit failed entirely, and frankly, freezing was preferable. At least he would go numb first and drift into sleep instead of feeling the burn in his lungs.

He had no illusions about being rescued. There was no telling when or if Rodgers would return; certainly, he would be more than happy to leave him here to suffer a slow and lonely death. A rescue from his crew was not going to happen; even if they had an available shuttle, neither of them had the ability to fly it through the dense minefield without adapters. And he was of absolutely no interest or value to the military forces currently swarming the Colanta system. They'd have much more urgent matters at hand, such as a rogue pirate vessel ready for combat, and potential dissidents within their ranks.

He didn't want to die. Not like this. Not when there was still something he had to do. As tempting as it would have been to give in to despair, to forgo the struggle and the pain, to simply close his eyes and drift away into the sweet embrace of nothingness, there was still that thing, that weapon, nestled in his bag, waiting for someone to stumble upon it long after he was gone. Whether it would be Rodgers or Archer or the Federation coming to claim the site after all the mess was sorted, somebody was bound to find it again. And he couldn't allow that to happen, even if it was the very last thing he did.

He rolled on his side, groaning at the pressure on his chest. Was he imagining it, or was it already getting more difficult to breathe? No, there had to be enough spare oxygen for a few more minutes, and he had to use those minutes wisely. Don't panic; ignore the pain.

He squinted as his gaze fell on Pearce's prostrate form, still and silent under the continuous onslaught of the lasers in the smaller chamber. There was no use for the man's punctured suit. But the one thing Pearce might provide was a functioning battery. Rodgers' blast had effectively taken out his own, rendering his suit ultimately useless, but thankfully the outer shell was still intact, and if he could switch the battery…it could buy him more time. He had to make the switch without making the situation even worse.

Of course, it was easier said than done. His knees almost gave way as he hauled himself up, and he had to pause, wheezing, so as not to pass out. When his head stopped spinning, he made a few careful steps toward the narrow door. His boots suddenly weighed more than the *Lisa*, and his vision was blurring along the edges. He was wasting precious air on nothing. The thought urged him on, step after step, until he was staring down at Pearce's body. He was lying facedown on the floor, his features obscured by the helmet, for which Matt was grateful.

He went down to his knees again, very carefully, praying he wouldn't pass out with the exertion. He reached carefully for Pearce's graviboot and pulled the dead man toward him, out of reach of the lasers. He had to pause to swallow down the nausea from the stabbing pain in his ribs.

The suit's battery was located at the back, just below the waist. As he detached it, the lights that were still flashing inside Pearce's helmet went out.

He reached behind his back. The battery was supposed to be easily removable even in this position. Of course, it would be easier when one had full control of their vision and fingers, in fully functional outer gear. As it was, Matt fumbled with the fastenings and the wiring for a few good minutes before he could make the switch. He was sucking in the last remaining oxygen, and his breathing sounded more like death rattles. His head was spinning, and his fingers, already swollen from before, felt like sausages inside the gloves. Focus. If he lost consciousness now, that was it.

The sudden flow of air as the new battery hooked in was overwhelming. It was sweet like a first kiss, like life itself. For a few minutes he sat there, taking deep breaths even though they hurt, filling his lungs, the oxygen clearing both his mind and his vision, awakening his dulled senses. The suit integrity alert came back on, along with the helmet light, but he ignored it for the moment. The important thing was that he wasn't going to suffocate immediately, and the suit was going to hold out long enough for him to do what he had to do.

He pushed himself up with great care and headed for the cannon plinth with renewed determination. The truly difficult part would be operating the damn cannon. Precision was absolutely crucial, and now he had to recreate the activation sequence from memory alone. Considering that he'd only glimpsed it from over Ryce's shoulder, he didn't have much to go on. He only hoped he'd retained enough of what Ryce had done, or all his efforts would be in vain.

Destroying the warhead had become a matter of principle by this point. If he had any time and energy to think about it, to consider all the unknowns in the equation, he might give up on the notion. The chances of his remembering the correct sequence were slim, and he didn't know where the cannon was aimed. He assumed it was pointing at the planet above, as Ryce had postulated, but he had no way of knowing for sure. The thing might not be in working order, or it might blow up in his face and take the entire moon with it. Which one it would be made little difference, really, considering he was about to die anyway.

Giving up would be easy. Nobody would blame him; nobody would even know about his dilemma. He'd always chosen to walk away from a fight rather than risk losing it. This shouldn't have been any different, but somehow it was. All the petty concerns fell away, dissipating into the darkness that surrounded him. All the things he'd craved so desperately in his life—freedom, recognition, independence, belonging—didn't matter anymore. The only thing that mattered, the only thing left to him was what he could do in these few final minutes, which would be more important than anything he'd done in his lifetime. Whoever these Mnirians had been, no matter how advanced their civilization, they were ultimately no better than humans. Was this really the pinnacle of achievement of any intellect—devising a method of killing that was so superior as to leave nothing but scorched earth in place of a thriving planet? Well, fuck them. All of them. Nobody had the right to wield such a weapon.

Ironically, the anger and the desperation strengthened his resolve. Focus, he told himself once more as he stared at the quiescent control panel. You can do it. He touched the blocks, and they glowed faintly, as if in welcome. He pushed harder, and they parted to reveal the receptacle cavity.

So far everything worked just as it had in the twin chamber what felt like eons ago. He let out a shaky breath and reached into his bag. The warhead was resting right there at the bottom of his kit, where it had been waiting as securely as it had on its pedestal throughout the centuries. It was heavy in his hands, much heavier than its four or five pounds. The effort of lifting and fitting it into the grooves inside the cavity was immense. Even with the renewed oxygen lifeline, he couldn't completely ignore his injuries. Blood pounded in his ears, and every breath felt like a hammer smashing against his ribs. But finally the thing was placed inside just so, and the control panel lit up in that familiar bluish glow.

Now came the hard part. Thankfully, the sequence Ryce had entered was short, and Matt had seen it in its entirety. As a pilot he was used to operating with long strings of numbers, translating digital data into three-dimensional environment. The order of touching the right symbols wouldn't have given him pause under different circumstances; whether he could reproduce it in his current condition was another matter.

Matt closed his eyes, recalling that sense of panic and urgency while standing there with Ryce. He was watching closely then. Start here with the lower left block, touching the symbol that resembled a hexagonal vortex, and continue on...

He opened his eyes and touched four symbols on four consecutive blocks in rapid succession, without giving himself an opportunity to pause and consider each move. There was a split second of anxiety when he was sure he'd done it all wrong, and then the blocks moved, forming a new arrangement around the warhead. He had to look away from the mounting intensity of the blue light. The walls and the floor shook slightly as an unseen mechanism kicked into gear.

The vibration, subtle as it was, threw him off balance. Matt clutched the top of the base plinth, narrowly avoiding the blocks, and slid down to the floor. He had enough presence of mind not to waste energy on cursing, but getting back up would put his dwindling physical resources to the test.

As before, in the second chamber, the six columns receded into the floor, carrying the paneled ceiling along with them. The opening in the roof slowly widened, offering a view of the solid rock encircling the silo and the scattering of dim pinpoints of light in the distance, and beyond– the barely visible disc of Colanta-3.

Matt didn't wait for the roof to open completely. He pushed himself up just enough to have a clear view of the etchings on the blocks, searching for the jumble of triangles that served as a "red button," and hit it with the palm of his hand.

The glow around the blocks became blinding, and even the faint light around the base of the cannon plinth intensified. Matt took that as a sign to get the hell out. He crawled away as fast as he could and cowered against the wall.

The blocks on the control panel collapsed inward, creating a solid partition, so Matt couldn't see what was happening to the warhead. The plinth, which seemed immovable before, rotated a few degrees on its axis, and the long barrel of the cannon protruded further into the round opening in the roof of the silo. There was a rough shaking in the stone, and suddenly, without further warning, the cannon went off, firing a burst of white flame into the void beyond. For a moment, all the lines and angles in the room stood out severely against the bleaching glare, and then in an instant, the shadows were back, gathering around the corners. The glow around the blocks dimmed, and the chamber was once again plunged into darkness, interrupted only by the flashing laser beams from the smaller chamber and his headlight.

Matt slumped against the wall, taking a shaky breath. That was it. He had no way of knowing if it had actually worked, or what would happen if it had. He'd done his best, and now there was nothing left to do but wait, either for death or… He didn't know what, exactly. But hope was a tenacious parasite, even when there was virtually nothing for it to feed upon.

Now, with the distraction of urgency gone, he could feel that the temperature had dropped. The oxygen was there, but the climate control had all but shut down. It probably wouldn't take long now. Val would know exactly how much, but Matt always sucked at the technical stuff. God, he hoped Val and Tony had gotten out of here with his *Lisa*. If the Fleet ships were occupied with dealing with the pirates, they stood a chance of slipping by unnoticed or taking cover until the storm blew over. And Ryce... Ryce had to come out of it alive somehow. He just had to, with his intellect, his idealism, his courage... It was gnawing at Matt's heart that he wouldn't know what had become of him, that he was left with this awful uncertainty. He'd never believed he could come to care so much for someone outside his little family, but there it was. And his being so helpless to save Ryce hurt more than all the broken bones in his body.

Oddly enough, he wasn't craving a drink right now; though, if there ever was a time for drinking himself into oblivion, it was now. He wasn't even really afraid of dying. Perhaps it was the numbness setting in, but all he could think about, besides the fate of his friends, was the feeling of sunshine and wind on his skin.

Matt closed his eyes, welcoming the memory. The cold was creeping up his spine, seeping into his bones, but he could almost feel the warmth of Earth's yellow sun on his face, the gentleness of his mother's kisses. That was the thing he regretted the most—not seeing her in those last few years, not going to her funeral. Naming his ship after her was an expression of remorse, but it didn't lessen how much he still missed her.

He couldn't feel his limbs anymore. It was going to be easy. As easy as falling asleep after a long, stressful day.

The floor under him shook a little, but he couldn't open his eyes even if he wanted to. His eyelids were heavy, and he was so tired. He was just going to rest his head on the grass and let the sound of the waves lull him into sleep.

Chapter Twenty

The sound of waves was soothing. They were crashing against the craggy shore in a never-ending rhythm, and he was floating, disembodied, on the sea breeze. Somebody was calling his name, the voice coming from far away, as incorporeal as he was. He didn't want to answer. It was so much easier to drift on the wind, without a care in the world. Somehow he knew that if he answered the voice, all the pain would come back.

"I know you can hear me," a stern female voice said in his ear.

"No, I can't," he mumbled, his eyes still firmly shut.

"You should be ashamed of yourself," the voice continued, with complete disregard for his denial. "I thought for sure you were dead, jackass."

By now, Matt kind of wished he were. He was slowly waking up from a blissful slumber to a room full of beeping monitors and glaring white lights. Surprisingly, he wasn't feeling any pain. He was a bit light-headed, like after a second or a third drink, which probably meant he was pumped full of analgesics, and he couldn't quite move. But at least he could breathe, and the cool recycled air had never been more welcome. He blinked sluggishly, taking it all in, and looked toward the source of the voice, which turned out to be Tony. She was sitting next to his bed, looking extremely sleep-deprived and bad-tempered.

It wasn't *Lady Lisa*'s makeshift infirmary, and it was too well equipped to be a maintenance station sickbay. He was lying on a wide hospital bed, with IV needles in his arms, surrounded by sleek and intimidating machines. There were three more beds in the room, but they were empty.

"Where am I?" he asked in a hoarse voice. He didn't remember anything after passing out in the cannon chamber.

"Aboard the *Lennox*," Tony said. She didn't sound too happy about it.

"What?" He tried to push himself up, wincing when the injured ribs twanged in warning.

The *Lennox* was Nora's command. Unless something had changed in the last two years, they were aboard his sister's ship. Rodgers hadn't mentioned the name of the Fleet destroyer that had shown up out of nowhere at the Colanta jumpgate, so this had to be it. Had they really rescued him from the bowels of the alien bunker?

"You must be the luckiest sod in the galaxy," Tony grumbled. "Even if you did miss out on all the action. I'll go get someone to have a look at you now that you're awake."

"No, wait." A sense of uneasiness settled over him now that he'd had a chance to take stock and reassure himself he really was alive and not hallucinating while slowly dying from oxygen deprivation. He was alive, but that was absolutely impossible. Tony was here, which probably meant Val was safe as well, but everything else was a big blur of uncertainty. "Where is Ryce?"

Tony looked troubled.

"Nora is here," she said, confirming his suspicions. "I think you better talk to her about it."

"Tony," he said. He was kind of proud of how calm he sounded. "Come on. If you know anything, just tell me. Where is he?"

"He's here," she said in exasperation. "Well, not *here* here. They took him out of the sickbay the second the doctors cleared him. He must be under arrest."

Matt plopped back on the pillow, shutting his eyes. Ryce was alive, at least. He didn't realize how tense he was until she said that. Despite the pressure of the bandages on his chest, it felt like he could suddenly take a full breath for the first time since seeing Ryce disappear into the dark tunnel with the pirate.

"So what happened?" Nora's ship, his rescue, Ryce's escape and recovery—it still made absolutely no sense. The events seemed disjointed, like a dream.

"Well, once you contacted us with your crazy-ass idea of surrendering yourself to the pirates, I reached out to Nora."

"How did you know how to contact her?" he asked suspiciously.

Tony simply looked at him.

"Okay, fine," he said tiredly. "Go on."

"Let me tell you, getting a hold of a senior Fleet officer for no other reason than her criminally inclined little brother has gotten himself into trouble again was no easy task."

"I'm not criminally inclined!" he protested. "I'm ambiguously resourceful."

"Do you want to hear the rest, or not?"

"Yes, sorry."

"Eventually I did get a hold of her, and we had a nice long chat about your predicament with this Rodgers character. Once she understood you were in real danger, she said she was coming right away. Then that D-cruiser appeared, and at first we thought it was her, but it just sat there and nothing happened. We kept spinning in orbit, keeping as close to the asteroid belt as we could, until the *Lennox* came in through the jumpgate. And if you're going to give me grief for calling your sister, Matt, I swear…"

"I'm not," Matt said hastily. "In case it wasn't already clear, I am grateful. In fact, I think I'll never doubt your wisdom again, hot stuff."

"Yeah, right," Tony said. "Anyway, Val and I went nuts worrying about you. They looked like they were ready to open fire on each other, and we had no idea where you were or what happened to you. And then, honestly, we almost forgot all about you, because it looked like the damn planet was going to explode."

"Oh, shit," Matt said. His hands shook with belated terror, and he clutched the sheets, struggling for control. How could he have been so stupid and shortsighted? How could he have forgotten that the *Lisa* was right there, orbiting Colanta-3, when he'd fired the alien weapon? He'd been so concerned with whether it was trained on the planet that he hadn't considered the danger of the blast wave hitting anything else in close proximity, like his own fucking ship. His only excuse was temporary mental incapacitation due to the lack of oxygen to his brain.

He must have gone white, because Tony asked in concern, "Are you okay?"

"Sure," he managed. "Fine. Did it? I mean, explode?"

"We probably none of us would be sitting here if it had," she said. "But there was some sort of explosion in the atmosphere, a big one. We weren't close enough, thank God, but we could see the flash of light and ripples in the clouds all along the planet surface. With everything that's been going on, I'm guessing you had something to do with that, didn't you?"

"It's a long story," he said. "But, yes."

"This is officially the worst job of my life," she complained. "And that includes the one that got me kicked off IMA."

"Trust me, it's not my shining moment either," Matt said, relaxing a fraction. Breathe. Everybody is okay.

"Frankly, I didn't know what to do. We thought for sure there was going to be a battle, but then the pirates just surrendered."

"Really?" Matt frowned. Surrender was not in Rodgers' character. He remembered how cool and collected the man had been facing the possibility of an attack by a Federation cruiser.

"Yes. I mean, what could they have done against two battleships? Maneuver as fast as they can, there was still no way they could slip past two Fleet ships into the jumpgate. And then, once all the hoo-ha was over, Nora—I should say Major Cummings—asked us to come on board. Well, ordered really. We didn't get to see much, but everybody was in a tizzy, and nobody could tell us anything until they brought you back. By then, I was absolutely frantic. Val too. Well, you know how he is, but trust me, he was frantic."

Matt smiled and squeezed her hand. "I'm sorry for causing you so much trouble. There goes your vacation on Nova, huh?" As much as he would have liked to continue talking to her, his eyelids felt heavy. The waves were calling to him again, and he wanted nothing more than to surrender to them. He was barely aware of Tony rising from her seat and gently kissing his forehead before the gentle dark took him.

☆☆☆

During the course of the next few days there wasn't much for him to do besides recuperate, which turned out to be incredibly boring. The medical staff was polite and professional, but for whatever reason, he wasn't allowed to use his commlink. Tony and Val came to see him two more times, which was the highlight of his stay. Unsurprisingly, there was no sign of Ryce, and nobody seemed to know what had happened to him. But Matt was healing quickly enough, considering the damage he'd sustained.

He was seriously considering making a break for it and heading to the canteen, when Nora came into the room, followed by a tall, broad-shouldered man with a commander's insignia on his army uniform.

Matt hadn't seen his older sister in more than four years. In uniform, with a severe haircut and a no-nonsense expression, she was the very image of their father in female form. Of course, she was much prettier, but there was no less ambition under that graceful exterior than there was in Fleet Admiral Thomas Cummings. Well, the Admiral could be proud of one of his children, at least, since the other one was such a spectacular failure.

"How are you doing?" Nora asked, sitting down on the edge of his bed.

Matt sat up with a sigh and lowered his feet to the floor. "I'm fine. Going a bit stir-crazy in here, though." He glanced at the commander, who was watching him with a stony expression. "Am I under arrest?"

"Not officially," Nora said, making herself more comfortable. "You are in custody until they figure out whether to charge you with anything. Such as illegally smuggling ancient artifacts in Federation space and defacing historic landmarks. Come on, Matt, how could you be so stupid as to get yourself mixed up in all this nonsense?"

"Are you sure you're not Tony's sister?" Matt muttered. "Because you sure sound a lot like her."

"Maybe you should listen to her more," Nora said. Considering they hadn't spoken in ages, she sure was falling back into the big sister act way too easily. "Sounds like she has a lot more sense than you."

"Yeah, I probably should," he said. And it probably wasn't going to happen, since they all knew how bad he was at taking advice. Even if it was good advice. Especially when it was good.

"This is Army Commander Walker," Nora said, gesturing toward the other man. Walker went as far as to grace him with a curt nod but otherwise remained silent. Matt felt an instant dislike. Though, to be fair, perhaps it was the commander's general demeanor to look disapproving, and nothing personal toward himself. Nora continued, "He was the leader of the task force that extracted you from the alien facility."

"Thanks," Matt said cautiously. It wasn't that he was ungrateful, but he was also pretty sure the man wasn't there to hear Matt gush over his daring rescue.

"Commander Walker would like to hear more from you regarding the Mnirian weapon you apparently launched at the planet," she said. "I told him he'd have your full cooperation."

"Sure," Matt said. It wasn't as though he had any choice, really, and he couldn't resist the vindictive urge to see Fleet brass fret about the careless destruction of their potential superweapon.

"With your permission, I'll drop in later to have a chat," Walker said. Most likely he wanted to question Matt without the inconvenience of his protective sister being present. "Ma'am."

Nora excused him and turned her full attention back to Matt, though she didn't speak right away.

"It's good to see you, Matthew," she said solemnly. "I wish it were under different circumstances. But I want you to know that I've missed you, and when I heard what had happened, I couldn't stand by and watch you get hurt."

Matt fidgeted. He looked up into her green eyes that conveyed nothing but sadness. He wasn't so sure anymore about his self-imposed separation from his family. Nora had naturally taken their father's side when Matt had announced he was quitting his military career. He'd been so wrapped up in his defiance that he hadn't stopped to think who else he was hurting. Like Nora. Like his mother. He'd always thought it was his father's fault he hadn't had a chance to say good-bye to her, but perhaps he had to admit some of the blame rested on him, too.

"I'm sorry you were dragged into this," he said. "It must be a hell of a mess to sort through."

"God, you have no idea," Nora said tiredly. "The pirates were apprehended and charged with kidnapping a Fleet officer, illegal scavenging, and attempted murder, not to mention a dozen other pending charges. But this whole crazy escapade of Archer's... I've informed Central Command. It's out of my hands now."

"What's going to happen to Archer?" he asked. It wasn't like he cared a great deal about the man; he was just building up his nerve to ask her about Ryce. He guessed he was the one who'd spilled the whole story about Archer's involvement, though why he would do that, considering his almost blind loyalty to the man, was beyond him. Ryce wasn't someone who'd save his own ass by betraying his comrades; that much he'd seen already.

"My guess? Nothing."

"Nothing?!" Matt forgot about his worry for Ryce for a second. "How could it be nothing? The man was planning to annihilate an alien home world using, yes, an illegally smuggled alien superweapon! And you're just letting him off the hook?"

"Look," Nora said mildly. "I'm not the one making the big decisions here. Do I think Archer deserves to get his ass kicked? Yes. Will he be reprimanded in some fashion? Most likely. But the man is a war hero, Matt. You know what he did in the Battle of Gunnar. And you don't put a war hero on trial in the middle of the actual war. It would damage morale; civilians don't need to see top officers dragged through the mud. They have to believe the Federation is there to protect them."

Matt huffed in annoyance. It was everything that infuriated him in the military. Apparently, a lot of shit could be swept under the carpet for the sake of projecting a solid image to the public and troops. It rankled that his own sister would be in support of that. But that's why they'd been estranged for so long, wasn't it? Nora was part of the system; she believed in it, while Matt despised its duplicity. And Nora wasn't nearly as unyielding in her judgment as their father. If he were here instead of her, he'd probably give Archer a damn medal and make sure Matt chilled in government prison for the next few years. But he wasn't here, and Nora, at least, was showing some sympathy for him, which, in all honesty, was probably more than he deserved.

"That's bullshit," he said, though he knew it sounded petulant. "Utter bullshit."

"At least you're alive to be angry about it," she pointed out. "Considering the mess you've been in. In fact, you've been incredibly lucky."

"Luck had nothing to do with it," Matt said. "Okay, maybe it had a little to do with it. But mostly it's Ryce I have to thank for being alive right now. Well, and you. And Commander Walker, apparently."

"Ryce?" Nora looked lost for a moment. "Oh, you mean Flight Lieutenant Easom. Faine's not his real name you know."

"Yeah, I figured." Matt pursed his lips. For some reason he felt awkward discussing him with her, but he had no other source of information. The ship personnel hadn't been very forthcoming in response to his questions. "Is he okay?"

"As well as can be expected," Nora said. "Don't quote me on any of this, but ultimately his fate depends on what happens to Archer. Easom is willing to give a full testimony, but there probably won't be a trial, and you can't charge an officer with criminal activity if everybody pretends nothing criminal had been going on. Even if Archer throws him to the wolves and denies any connection, CenCom would want to avoid the possibility of the allegations leaking out. He'd have a hard time denouncing Easom though, seeing as he was the one who'd alerted him to your situation directly and so was responsible for Archer arriving at Colanta. But either way, his military career is as good as over."

Matt's heart sank. It was ultimately Archer and Ryce's own fault for coming up with and carrying out the risky scheme, not to mention apparently communicating behind his back, but he couldn't help but feel responsible for how it had all gone downhill. If it hadn't been for Rodgers' obsession with him, Archer would have his precious leverage against the Alraki, and Ryce would have his illustrious career as a combat pilot. Everybody would be happy. Except him, perhaps, since he was reasonably sure Archer wouldn't let him run around with this kind of knowledge.

"Can I see him?"

"I'm not sure that's a good idea."

"Nora, please," Matt said. "I'll send you a box of chocolate almonds for your birthday. You still like those, right?"

She let out a heavy sigh. "You're impossible, you know that? Okay, fine, you can see him. For a few minutes. He was the one who went in with Walker to search for you, after all."

"He did?" Matt couldn't quite name the warmth that spread in his chest. He wished he could ignore it, since it was making him uncomfortable.

"Yes. After the pirates surrendered and we had him in custody, he insisted on going in, which actually proved a great help. He was the only one who knew how to use that laser device we'd confiscated from Rodgers. I wasn't there, but Walker said it was a hell of an operation. You must have had quite an impact on him, for him to disregard his own injuries to save you." She touched his hand. "But I'm glad he did. I was told it was a matter of minutes before brain damage would have been irrevocable. If Walker had had to go in blindly, you'd be dead for sure."

Matt looked away. There were too many emotions clamoring inside him, and he wasn't sure he was ready to face them. Part of him wanted to forget everything that had happened, all the fear and despair. And part of him wanted to savor every moment, to remember that despite everything, he was alive. And yes, he was lucky. Because he had his ship, his friends, a sister, and somebody who apparently cared for him enough to risk his own life to help save him.

"Thank you for rushing to my defense," he said, to change the topic to something less disturbing. "A whole destroyer, just for me. I should be honored. Hope you won't get in trouble for wasting the Fleet's resources like that. But you could always pull a secret Mnirian military base out of your hat to turn everything to your advantage, right?"

"There's always that," Nora smiled, but it didn't quite reach her eyes.

It looked like he had good reason to worry, but there was nothing he could do about it at this point. He said nothing to Nora, but he hoped the underground base didn't hold any more nasty surprises. Archer might have lost his chance to implement his intimidation tactic, but Matt knew all too well there were far worse decisions made every day in CenCom headquarters. And he preferred not to supply them with any more weapons than they already had at their disposal.

Chapter Twenty-One

After a couple of days, Matt was transferred from the sickbay into a holding cell. It wasn't uncomfortable, as cells went; in fact, it was larger than the passenger cabins on *Lady Lisa*. It was clean, well-lit, and had its own en suite shower, so he didn't mind crashing there for the moment. The uncertainty and the wait were much worse than the accommodations. He was still in bandages and still aching all over, but having received proper care, he was healing quickly. The broken ribs were fusing back together, and he was so pumped with various drugs that his dreams were blissfully blank. He could have used a drink or two, but the need was distant and dull-edged.

Nora dropped in a couple more times, but she seemed preoccupied and less forthcoming, so he guessed that despite her assurances to the contrary, she was under quite a lot of pressure. He did his best not to push her, but continuously being in the dark was driving him bonkers. Tony and Val were not allowed to see him now that he was nearly fully recovered. He almost wished they would charge him with something so he could spill all the dirt during the trial, though of course he wasn't really naive enough to believe that would change anything, especially if the top brass had already decided to play down the incident.

He was also bored out of his mind. He had very limited, and no doubt monitored, web access, and no open-news source had mentioned anything about Colanta, not even the apprehension of a wanted pirate. Not that he expected anything else, really. If his sister hadn't been the one to hold them, he would have been seriously concerned about his and his crew's safety. But he couldn't picture Nora supporting the elimination of her own brother as a troublesome witness. Granted, a lot could have changed in a few years, especially when ambitious high-ranking officers were involved, but she'd always been honest to a fault, and far less politically oriented than their father. So he bit down on his impatience and waited meekly for any updates.

Being questioned by Commander Walker was the only thing that brought a bit of excitement to Matt's life. Under different circumstances, the commander would have been easy on the eyes, but recently, Matt had developed an aversion to chiseled jaws and forceful attitudes. On his side, Walker did a poor job of concealing his derision for a man he clearly considered little more than a traitor. It certainly made for an interesting encounter. Matt almost regretted his promise to Nora to be cooperative, but he duly recounted everything that had happened since being hired by the taciturn Mr. Ari. And then recounted it again and again, as Walker picked at every little detail.

He couldn't tell if his account was something Walker wanted to hear or not, but he decided he would be truthful. He didn't even dodge the questions regarding his contracts with Pat Gentry, figuring he was in as much trouble as he could possibly be already. The only thing he left out was his relationship with Ryce, if one could call it a relationship. It wasn't relevant, and it definitely wasn't Walker's business.

In addition to the details of his unfortunate recruitment, he was questioned ad nauseam about the Mnirian base and what he'd done to fire the weapon, by both Walker and Fleet Intelligence officers. Unsurprisingly, no one told him whether they'd found anything else of value in the bunker. He didn't really want to know anyway. His single heroic act notwithstanding, some things were best forgotten as quickly as possible.

He couldn't stop worrying about Ryce, but he didn't ask about him anymore. His inquiries were bound to make things worse for the pilot, who was already in a precarious situation. So he waited and tried to focus on his recuperation, since there was little else he could do.

It felt like weeks, though only a few days had passed since he'd met with Nora. They were still stationed in the Colanta system, ostensibly waiting for CenCom to reach a decision about the matter. Apparently, the Fleet wasn't taking any more risks where the Mnirian facility was involved.

So when the door of his cell opened with no prior warning, admitting a uniformed sergeant, he wasn't expecting it.

"Mr. Spears, come with me," the sergeant said dryly.

Matt had been reclining on his bunk, and he wasted no time getting up to follow his escort out of the cell and into the long empty corridor. His heart was pounding, but he didn't want his sudden nerves to show.

He mustn't have been considered a menace or a flight risk, given he had only one guard.

He was led a few levels down, into the higher security area of the holding bay. There was nothing overtly oppressive about the plain gray of the corridor, but the rows of locked doors put him on edge. Being cooped up on a tiny ship but still having the ability to decide its course was a far cry from being stuffed into a tiny cell, stripped of any semblance of choice.

They stopped in front of a door, and the sergeant punched in a code on the touch lock. The door slid aside, revealing a plain white cell with a single bunk and a facility closet.

Ryce looked up from where he was sitting on the bunk. His guarded expression changed.

"You have half an hour," the sergeant said. He let Matt inside, and the door closed softly after him. There was an awkward moment of silence.

Ryce looked good. The pain-induced gauntness was gone from his face. The only reminder of his injuries was a white bandage on his left wrist. But when he easily pushed himself to the edge of the bunk, he appeared able to use his arm freely, so at least there was no permanent damage. He studied Matt carefully, probably admiring the swirling shades of green and yellow the fading bruises had left on his face, but he made no move to greet him.

"So, um," Matt said when the silence stretched. "Thanks for getting me out, I guess."

Ryce shrugged. "I merely showed the way. Truthfully, I was sure they were going to recover your dead body, but I couldn't leave you there, even if it were true."

"You didn't have to do it," Matt replied.

"Neither did you," Ryce said. "But you did."

There was another pause.

"I didn't know you had a major for a sister," Ryce said. His tone was neutral, but Matt imagined he could hear an accusatory note in his voice. "She thanked me, too."

"We haven't been keeping in touch lately," he said. "What's going to happen to you now? Are you going to be court-martialed?"

"I've made it very clear that if I were to stand trial, Archer would too," Ryce said. He still hadn't moved from the bunk. "And he hasn't actually denied anything. It would be a publicity debacle the Fleet can't afford right now. So I'm guessing it'll be a quiet discharge."

Matt's hands curled into fists involuntarily. It wasn't fair. Ryce was a fucking genius; he had a spectacular career ahead of him. And now it was all over, because of what? Archer's God complex, Matt's shitty choices in business associates, Ryce's own excessive integrity, or pure and simple bad luck? Either way, he must have felt as if his world was crumbling down, and here they were, barely able to look each other in the eye.

"I still don't think he was entirely wrong, actually," Ryce continued, ignoring Matt's expression. "The war's been going on for too long, and we're yet to gain any sort of strategically significant advantage. The Mnirian weapon could have given us leverage. But it wasn't meant to be used merely as leverage, was it?"

He paused and looked away for a moment, and then continued in a weary tone: "I'm done lying. They can sort it all out without me."

"I'm sorry," Matt said. It was such a little thing to say, but there was nothing else he could offer.

"Don't be. I'm sorry you got involved in this. I'm aware that in your line of work you don't need such complications."

That threw Matt off. He didn't view it that way; it was his fault the job had turned sour, not Ryce's. It suddenly dawned on him that they had such a short time, and here they were wasting it on offering each other carefully worded apologies and regrets, when in actuality, they needed to say something far more important.

"Fuck that," Matt said fiercely. The cell most likely had video feed, but he was done caring. "Look, I know you don't operate like regular people. At least not in the way I'm used to. But back there, when you kissed me...did you mean it?"

It had been just one kiss. Normally, he wouldn't have given it a second thought. Kisses meant nothing, sex meant nothing; even the few casual relationships he'd managed to have before choosing to become a free agent meant nothing. But this was Ryce, and Ryce was different in every sense of the word. Under other circumstances, he wouldn't have dared to ask him this, but it seemed as though neither of them had anything to lose anymore.

Their future, their freedom, hung in the balance, and he wanted to be certain there was something there other than his wishful thinking, even if higher powers chose to tear them apart again. No more regrets, no more what-ifs. He was done losing people because his head was so firmly lodged in his ass he couldn't bring himself to tell them he cared. How many years had he lost with Nora? How much time had he spent fuming at his mother, despite her attempts to reconcile, before the opportunity was lost forever? He couldn't afford to do it now, not when he was feeling... He wasn't sure exactly what he was feeling, but he didn't need words to define it. He just wasn't ready to give up on it.

"Yes," Ryce said, looking up at him and catching his gaze. And with that single word Matt's world was changed forever, broken and mended at the same time. "I did mean it."

He glanced upward, where the hidden camera must have been located, and shook his head, probably coming to the same conclusion regarding possible spectators.

"It's not something I've felt before," he continued with unusual frankness. "I didn't want to feel it. We're too different, too...incompatible. It goes without saying it would never have worked between us, and not because I was a Fleet officer and you were—are—a smuggler." He stared down at his hands. Matt suddenly realized he'd never seen Ryce so unsure of himself. Perhaps Matt hadn't been the only one to wonder whether the other party was on the same page.

"But when we were limping back to the shuttle after you'd pulled me out of the silo, that's when I knew it didn't matter. I knew that I'd be set adrift if I lost you."

Matt's throat closed. Ryce had been true to his word. He'd done everything he could to save him, including playing gambits with a psychopathic killer and ending any prospects he might have had to rise through the Fleet hierarchy. It left him dizzy with the sheer inconceivability of it.

There was only one thing Matt could do now. He took Ryce's good hand and pulled him up, so they were standing face-to-face, their bodies almost touching. He was acutely aware of the other man, the warmth of his body radiating through the coarse fabric of the prison jumpsuit, the smell of the cheap military-issue shampoo in his hair.

"It's unfair we only got half an hour," he murmured, lifting his hand to trace the clean outline of Ryce's jaw.

"Then you'll have to make it up to me when there's no one watching," Ryce said, and leaned in for a kiss.

☆☆☆

"You're one lucky son of a bitch," Tony said for the hundredth time. Val grunted in agreement.

They were standing in the D3-4 terminal of the *Lennox*, waiting for *Lady Lisa* to be cleared for takeoff. They could see her from their position on the railed catwalk that ran around the perimeter of the terminal. Their tiny vessel was further dwarfed by the huge expanse of the docking bay, and her ungainly Phaeton form was incongruous amidst the sleek modern facilities. The Fleet destroyer was easily as large as some space stations and held nearly as many people. The cargo vessel terminal demonstrated this very well, as it was designed to accommodate much larger ships than the *Lisa*. As soon as the security team currently scanning her gave the all clear, they'd be free to leave.

Matt wasn't thrilled about letting military personnel take liberties with his ship; in fact, he was planning on sending Val on a mission to search for potential bugs the moment they stepped on board. But Nora had been adamant about the security service wiping the *Lisa* clean before they went on their way, and that meant making sure their cargo hold was empty of any and all goods, and that the computer logs were deleted. Matt was certain he could reproduce the flight data from memory, but appearances had to be upheld, it seemed.

Tony was right, though. He really was lucky, and he harbored no illusions as to why he was being released without so much as a slap on the wrist. Nora must've pulled some serious strings to get him off the hook for criminal and possibly treason charges. Tony had hinted that his father, the almighty Admiral Cummings, had a hand in this as well, but Matt dismissed the idea. If anything, Nora might have gone against the Admiral's wishes. His father would have loved nothing more than for the prodigal son to spend some time in a correctional facility, reflecting on his unfortunate life choices.

Matt had to admit most of his recent choices had been regrettable. Ironically, he had managed to go against his better judgement on every major decision that had led him to this point, starting with taking this damn job in spite of his gut feeling. Worse, he'd been so set against taking the weapon out of its underground repository—and yet he'd been the one to ultimately use it. He still couldn't contemplate it without breaking out in cold sweat. Though Colanta-3 appeared to be completely barren, there was no way of knowing for sure if some primordial microorganisms hadn't begun their long journey to someday evolving into intelligent creatures—a potential that Matt had single-handedly destroyed.

That thought was extremely disconcerting. This was the last time he'd let himself be blinded by greed enough to ignore obvious red flags.

"I think they're done," Val said. He was leaning on the railing, watching intently as a uniformed team descended from the airlock ramp of the *Lisa* onto the tarmac. Val was probably even more pissed than Matt at somebody touching his baby.

"Good," Matt said. "Let's get out of here already."

He stepped away from the railing, wincing at the twinge of discomfort in his ribs. The bones had mended, but he was still aching and tended to be reminded of it with every incautious movement.

The three of them headed toward the staircase, but halted as an armed convoy showed up on the catwalk right below them. The security guards glanced at them suspiciously, but Matt's attention was drawn to their prisoner, and he gripped the railing so hard his knuckles turned white.

Feeling his gaze, Rodgers looked up and smirked as he saw him. He didn't look like a man who was facing justice for his crimes. In fact, he looked kind of smug. He slowed and waved at Matt with his cuffed hands.

"You're like a fucking cat, Spears, always landing on your feet. Be careful, you're running out of lives."

"At least I'm not the one who's gonna stare at the walls for the rest of his life," Matt retorted, though the veiled threat didn't go unnoticed. He had no doubt that even incarcerated, Rodgers had the ability to cause him a lot of trouble.

"You're not the only one with friends in the right places," Rodgers said.

"Move along," the guard said, nudging Rodgers with his weapon. "You can send love letters to each other later."

Rodgers threw him a murderous look, made even more sinister by the eye patch. The convoy proceeded down into the docking bay, presumably to catch a prison transport vessel. Matt didn't release the railing until they were safely out of sight.

"What did he mean by that?" Tony frowned.

"What do you think he meant?" Matt headed down the stairs. Rodgers' words had rattled him, and a deep sense of unease settled somewhere deep within his chest. Thinking back, even when confronted with Archer and his ultimatum, Rodgers hadn't seemed worried by the possibility of an open confrontation with a Fleet cruiser. Matt didn't like the implications of that. If Rodgers somehow managed to wiggle his way out of this…he was in serious trouble. Pat Gentry's viciousness had nothing on Rodgers', not when he'd already missed the chance to nail Matt to the wall twice.

His anxiety slipped to the back of his mind as they approached *Lady Lisa*. He tapped his adapters, creating an instant link with the ship, and the main hatch opened invitingly. Matt lovingly patted her battered side. Drifting in close proximity to the asteroid belt had left a few new bumps on the hull. Sure, now that they'd lost Mr. Ari's fee, they couldn't afford the more expensive upgrades, but this was nothing Val's capable hands and a few licks of paint couldn't fix. For him, she was still the most beautiful ship in the galaxy, the only place he could call home. Going up the ramp for the first time in what felt like months was like returning to a mother's embrace. When he'd bought her all those years ago, he had still been reeling at the estrangement from his family, angry and hurting. But true to her name, she'd kept him safe ever since. She was his anchor, preventing him from being cast adrift into the endless night.

The sentiment echoed what Ryce had told him the last time Matt had seen him. Spoken in the confines of a holding cell, the words had struck a chord but hadn't fully set in. Matt had never thought of himself as a person to inspire such feelings in anyone. If anything, he was the one people wanted to get rid of, as demonstrated by his father.

If he were a smart man, he'd run. As fast and as far as he possibly could. Away from any entanglements, familial or adversarial. He'd changed his name once; he could do it again if necessary. But as much as he yearned to escape the unwanted attention of both his father and Rodgers, he also yearned to belong. To one place, one name, one person. And astonishingly, inexplicably, that person was Ryce. He knew with absolute clarity he would never run away from Ryce, even if it meant giving up his freedom and the life he'd worked so hard to build for himself. Because he…

Yeah. He wasn't smart, that's for sure.

Tony and Val disappeared inside, and he lingered on the ramp, waiting. He didn't know for what, exactly. Nora had already said her good-byes, along with a stern admonition to keep in touch with her. Ryce was probably still in his cell, and Rodgers, hopefully, was well on his way to a maximum security facility.

He looked up at the long narrow screen above the docking bay pressure doors. From this vantage point, he couldn't see the lifeless planet, the deadly asteroids, or the red sun. There were only stars, as pure and as distant as ever.

Matt sighed and ducked into the airlock.

"Okay, guys. Let's go find us another job."

Epilogue

If you've seen one maintenance station canteen, you've seen them all.

Matt came to this brilliant conclusion as he casually sipped his piss-awful beer at Messa-1 station's popular (and only) watering hole, the Red Fog. The decor was expectedly understated, and the menu was terrifying, but he wasn't here for fine wining and dining.

As he waited, the patrons that were there when he arrived finished their drinks and left one by one, replaced by freshly tired faces as the day shift ended. Matt ordered his third beer, resisting the urge to check the clock again.

A Freeport would have made a better rendezvous spot, but he did his best to avoid major points of registration for now. After abandoning his base of operations (such as it was) in the Sonora sector, he'd chosen a quieter stomping ground here at Elysium. Sure, the jobs were scarcer and less lucrative than in one of the major systems, but here, he had fewer chances of being ratted out to the wrong people.

They had been keeping a low profile for the last six months. While it had been tough at times making ends meet, so far they hadn't encountered any trouble, neither with the Feds nor with less law-abiding personages. Matt had been monitoring the news religiously, eager for any tidbit of information regarding Rodgers and the *Black Baza*, but there was none. That didn't mean anything, really. Sensitive information, like that pertaining to the possible release of a known pirate, wouldn't leak out to the public if the Feds could help it. And somebody like Rodgers would have plenty of outside contacts while serving time. So considering the risks, Matt's crew was totally on board with his relocation choices, even if it meant getting considerably lower wages for the foreseeable future.

Matt frowned at the empty bottle in front of him. He contemplated ordering another, but decided against it. The beer really wasn't any good, and if he were going back to the ship on his lonesome tonight, it wouldn't be enough to get him drunk anyway.

He pushed the empty bottle aside. He'd wait another ten minutes. He wasn't sure if he should feel worried or slighted. The meeting had been set up weeks ago, via a curt message, and a lot could have gone wrong in the interim.

The minutes ticked by, both excruciatingly slowly and way too fast, each one slipping away like a missed opportunity. Finally, he sighed heavily and stood up, swiping the tabletop to pay. This had been a mistake. Nobody joined his crew if they had other prospects, and a combat pilot, even an ex-combat pilot discharged under questionable circumstances, would always have plenty of other more lucrative and way more legal prospects. And as much as Matt loved to flatter himself, chances were that whatever mysterious appeal he had held for Ryce had dissipated over six long months of detention.

He turned to leave and stopped in his tracks. Ryce stood in the doorway with a large duffel bag slung over his shoulder. He looked almost the same as the first time Matt had seen him—the proud posture, the perfect features; except now, there was a hardness in his gaze and fines lines etched the corners of his mouth.

He was the most beautiful sight in the galaxy.

Ryce spotted him, and his face lit up. He crossed the floor of the small canteen in a few long strides.

"So," Matt said, trying for nonchalance even though he knew he had a stupid grin plastered all over his face. "Coming in for your job interview, Mr. Easom?"

Ryce arched an eyebrow.

"Are there lots of other contenders for the position?"

"Absolutely none." Matt pulled him into a hug, oblivious to the stares of the other patrons. "I thought you wouldn't come," he whispered, the words tentative and barely audible.

Instead of an answer, Ryce dropped his bag and drew Matt into an unexpected, fierce kiss. The desperate, overwhelming rawness of it left them both breathless and struggling for control.

Ryce took half a step back, his eyes bright and locked on Matt's. Something that had been lodged deep inside Matt, festering like a splinter in an open wound, shifted, lessening the dull ache that up until now was so much a part of him. He let himself open up to the promise in those gray eyes, and suddenly it was hard to breathe around the lump in his throat.

"You taste like beer," Ryce said, wrinkling his nose.

"And you taste"—like starlight, Matt wanted to say, but settled for—"like an arrogant asshole."

"You would know," Ryce said, but the corners of his mouth twitched in a smile. "So I gather you've given up on your immutable rule of not shitting where you eat."

"It was a stupid rule anyway." Matt picked up the bag, threw an arm around Ryce's shoulders, and guided him toward the exit. *Lady Lisa* was waiting at the docks, ready for takeoff as soon as her captain returned with the newest addition to the crew.

"You know, Mr. Easom, or whatever the hell your name is," Matt said. "I think you're gonna fit right in."

About the Author

A voracious reader from the age of five, Isabelle Adler has always dreamed of one day putting her own stories into writing. She loves traveling, art, and science, and finds inspiration in all of these. Her favorite genres include sci-fi, fantasy, and historical adventure. She also firmly believes in the unlimited powers of imagination and caffeine.

Twitter: https://twitter.com/Isabelle_Adler
Website: http://www.isabelleadler.com
Email: info@isabelleadler.com

NINESTAR PRESS, LLC

www.ninestarpress.com

Printed in Great Britain
by Amazon

87620544R00112